MW00880808

AN INJURED RACCOON FROM THE FUTURE...

A SHY GIRL...

A MISSION TO SAVE THE PLANET...

BUT SOMETHING WASN'T RIGHT.

Ricky thought he was prepared for anything. But he soon learned that a broken leg, an overly protective cat, and vindictive squirrels were the least of his worries.

His mission was simple - save three targets in order to change the fate of the world and all of humanity. Those three targets were so important to the future of animals that he couldn't wait to meet them.

Only they were the stuff of nightmares...

A butcher, a hunter, and a scientist, all treating animals in the most horrible ways.

Was this really the mission, or was there some kind of mistake? What should he do?

The adventure begins!

Published by: Trash Panda Books - Woodbridge, Connecticut

    www.TrashPandaBooks.com

Cover Art by: Echo Chernik

    www.echo-x.com

Additional Illustrations by: Echo Chernik and Kent Golden

Text Design by: Kent Golden

Library of Congress Control Number: 2019919289

First Edition

RICKY
THE TIME TRAVELING TRASH PANDA

by
KENT GOLDEN

Woodbridge, CT

For *all* of the animals.

(humans included.)

CONTENTS

PROLOGUE: THE HOSPITAL

November 8th, 2014
Connecticut, USA

*E*mma Gregor was staring out of the window of the hospital waiting area, watching some squirrels frolicking on the grassy area down below near the road. There were so many of them! Just when she thought she had counted them all, two more came bouncing out of the green hedges that lined the sidewalk. Busy pedestrians walked right by, but the squirrels remained unphased. These were city squirrels – they held their ground like knights defending a castle keep. Especially when food was involved. Some kind benefactor must have left behind part of their lunch and the squirrels were swarming the area in a fuzzy gray and brown blur.

A few feet away in the waiting area, an older gentleman coughed a little, put down his magazine and looked towards her. He lifted his bushy white eyebrows and stretched his neck to look out of the window and down in the general direction she was facing.

"You look pretty intense over there young lady," he said without turning towards her. "If I may be so bold, what are you looking at?"

At first, Emma shied away a little and ran her fingers through her brown hair, pushing a few stray strands over her ear. Her bright green eyes eventually turned towards the man. She saw that he had white hair and dark skin with small spots on his cheeks that reminded Emma of Morgan Freeman, one of her favorite actors.

"Just watching the squirrel channel," she said quietly with a slight smile. That's what her mom always called it.

The man cackled a bit and his gaze turned towards her. "Oh, that one's my favorite!" he said as his face lit up and softened with dozens of wrinkles around his eyes. "My wife and I used to watch that all the time. She used to get after me when I would feed all of our crackers and peanut butter to them. Now it's just me, but I still enjoy it." She could see his eyes darting around as he looked back out of the window and followed the furry antics outside.

Emma took a moment to glance at the man as he looked out of the window. She wondered how long ago it was that he lost his wife. Was there a set timeframe for getting over such a thing? Emma looked down at her small stuffed raccoon keychain that her mom had given her and turned it over and over in her hands nervously.

"My wife used to say that the animals of the world are way smarter than we give them credit for. You can see it sometimes, ya know?" the man said.

Emma's curiosity was piqued, and she stopped fiddling with the soft fur of the keychain. "What do you mean?"

"Well, sometimes you catch them in the act. Take that hot dog stand down there for example…" he was about to continue but paused when he heard the nearby door open.

A female nurse in maroon scrubs came out with a clipboard.

"Mr. Delman?" she asked, looking around the room. Emma and this man were the only ones there, and she thought it was pretty obvious that she wasn't Mr. Delman, but the nurse must have been following some protocol that you not assume who anyone was.

"Oh, over here!" the man said, holding his finger up in the air as if he had just won a prize.

"Sorry, duty calls," he said cheerfully as he got up and headed towards the nurse.

"Nice chatting with you," he said vaguely in her direction as he followed the nurse out of the room.

Emma was sorry to see him go, since he was a good distraction from the reason for her being here in the hospital: Mom.

A short distance away, down the bright white halls that smelled of disinfectant, her dad was busy talking with the doctors. A little while ago they had told her she should leave the room for a bit.

Emma protested, pointing out that she was eleven years old now and could handle it. She wanted to know what was going on with Mom too. But her dad had agreed with the doctors. He would be out soon and relay the status update to her. Seeing as she didn't have much choice in the matter, she reluctantly agreed. She mused that maybe in a few years once she got into high school, she would have more control over her own life.

So here she sat under pulsing fluorescent lights, trying not to think about what they might be talking about. She was no fool, Mom was in rough shape and getting worse.

Emma forced her attention back onto the squirrels. What was that man talking about with the hot dog cart? She squinted her eyes against the bright sunlight and patiently observed the scene down below. A vendor was selling hot dogs and pretzels from a small silver cart with a colorful red and yellow umbrella on top. Steam rolled out from a deep tray as the man removed a silver cover and used long tongs to pull out three plump, reddish hot dogs. He lifted them out and pushed them expertly into buns for a mother and her two kids.

The customer handed off the hot dogs to the children and worked on juggling her own whilst getting her wallet out to pay for it all.

Then Emma thought she saw something on the left edge of the cart - some motion near the rotating tower of salted pretzels. It was a silver and glass enclosure with a red heat lamp at the top that kept the huge pretzels hot and crispy. She remembered eating ones just like it at the zoo last year with Mom. Maybe it was just the rotating mechanism she saw? Or maybe a pretzel fell off its little hook?

On the right side of the cart, the hot dog man was patiently waiting for the woman to pay. Only the woman was distracted by a squirrel that was getting very close to one of the kids. It had leapt up to a bench and was reaching out with its little paws for their food. Emma could see the kid pointing at the squirrel excitedly as if it were the coolest thing it had ever seen. Now the other kid was joining in and the three of them were laughing and leaning over as if to have a conversation with the furry panhandler. They handed off a few morsels of their bread and you could see their delight as it took it right from their hands.

"Yeah, that's pretty cute I guess," Emma said to herself. "They've learned how to scam the humans for a few crumbs. Good for you, guys."

She exhaled almost with a little disappointment and started to turn away from the window when she noticed more movement on the other side of the cart. As if by magic, the glass door of the pretzel tower was slowly opening on its own.

Emma quickly looked to see if the hot dog man had noticed, but he was oblivious. The door then stopped moving. Maybe the wind had blown it open?

A moment later, she saw a pretzel slowly raise up off of its hook and disappear over the back side of the cart.

"What the…?" she said out loud with a tinge of amazement in her voice. On the other side, the woman paid for the food and the three of them continued their meal on the bench. The hot dog vendor put the cash in his drawer and proceeded to re-stock some of the chips and sodas at the front of the cart. Emma kept watching, but her sense of wonder started to fade when nothing else happened.

A few moments later, she was startled when the door from the hallway opened again and her dad came out with a serious look on his face. She slid away from the window to face him and gently stuffed the furry keychain into her pocket.

"Hey honey," he said as he walked over slowly. Emma knew right away the news wasn't good. A rising sense of panic was building in her that she couldn't control, but she made sure to not show it outwardly.

He held out his hand for her as he got closer. "Let's go for a walk."

Emma didn't know what to think. She didn't take his hand but instead got up on her own. They started to walk down one of the long hallways together.

"What did they say?" she finally managed to ask.

Her dad took a deep breath as if it would help him come up with the right way to answer her. "It's as we feared. She doesn't have long."

Emma knew this moment would come at some point and was afraid she might burst into tears, but instead she felt numb.

Her dad continued. "I know this must be difficult for you. It's difficult for me too. But there's really nothing we can do about it."

"I know," she said. She could feel her heart pounding in her chest with the surge of adrenaline that was flowing through her entire body. Her hands were shaking a bit and felt cold and clammy even though the rest of her body felt hot.

"I want you to talk to someone. It doesn't have to be me, but I want you to talk to someone about all of this so that you don't bottle it all up inside. Until we can find a good professional, maybe one of your friends from school?"

Emma looked down at her feet as they walked. She didn't really have any friends from school.

"How about that girl Monique that you and mom were talking about last month?" her dad asked.

Emma surprised herself when she smiled a little.

"Yeah, I can talk to Monique. She's really good at listening."

Her Dad stopped walking and crouched to face her in the hallway. "Ok, good. I'm here for you too," he said sincerely.

"I know, Dad. Thanks."

He did his best to smile and gave her a big hug. "Let's stop

Ricky the Time Traveling Trash Panda | 13

home for dinner and we can come back later tonight. Your mom is resting right now anyway."

Emma nodded in silent agreement.

They walked together towards the main lobby of the hospital. The walking seemed to help calm her down a little. As they emerged into the bright light outside, Emma inhaled the smell of cooking hot dogs and glanced over towards the vendor with the cart. The woman and the two kids were gone. The pretzel tower continued its slow rotation under the warm glow of the red heat lamp. She couldn't see any empty hooks – they all had pretzels waiting for the next customers.

As they continued towards the parking garage, Emma noticed one of the bushes next to the exterior stairs moving slightly. She stopped in her tracks and slowly moved closer a step at a time. Her dad hadn't noticed and kept walking. Finally, she crouched down to get a look under the dense green foliage of the bush.

It was then that she saw a rather plump looking gray squirrel chowing down on a half-eaten pretzel. Even with half of it gone it was still huge and looked comically large in its tiny paws. After a moment its eyes got wide as if it knew she was watching. In a flash both the squirrel and the pretzel were gone.

"Emma, sweetie? You ok?" her dad was asking from a few feet away to her side.

"Uh, yeah. Just tying my shoe. Be right there."

She looked for a few more seconds to see if she could tell where the squirrel had gone, but it had left no trace.

"Well played, little guys," she said with respect.

"Well played."

PART ONE: THE ARRIVAL

CHAPTER ONE: *RICKY*

"Is it safe?" Ricky asked with a hint of trepidation. He risked a glance at Rupert, the other raccoon in the lab who was a few feet away tapping quickly at an illuminated control panel. Soft beeps sounded with each touch and colorful readouts glowed in stark contrast to the otherwise mirror black surfaces.

"Safe?" Rupert asked in reply while still working the controls. "Safe is a relative term," he said dryly.

That wasn't exactly the answer that Ricky was hoping for, especially since he was now standing inside the accelerator chamber about to make a time jump into the unknown past. A faint and rhythmic humming sound was making his long whiskers vibrate.

The chamber was a small hexagonal shaped compartment made of non-reflective slate gray metal. Ricky looked down at his black raccoon feet and wiggled his toes as if to make sure they were really his and he wasn't dreaming or something. He looked at the corners of the chamber and all around the cramped space. In the seams there were strips of white light that glowed softly from the floor to the ceiling. He reached out with his black paws and felt around gingerly at the smooth walls.

"Don't touch anything," Rupert said firmly.

"Oops. Sorry!" Ricky said apologetically, pulling his paws back to his reddish-brown fur. He didn't even know Rupert could see him from out there. He made sure to pull his striped tail closer to his body so that it wouldn't touch in the back.

His furry black masked face scrunched up as he tried to see one of Rupert's many screens along the wall and an angled workstation area. There must have been a video feed of the chamber interior displaying on one of them. It was unnerving to have your every movement under scrutiny.

Ricky took a deep breath to try and center himself. A faint smell of sterilizer filled his nose and he tried to remember the last time he ate something. That was yesterday afternoon. They had told him that an empty stomach would be best, but his stomach kept telling him otherwise.

He looked across the room and saw a large red circle glowing on the wall. Well, it was almost a circle, anyway. There was a small gap at the top that was getting smaller. He knew from his training that it was the countdown. It was almost time.

"Here is your wristband," Rupert said as he held out the silvery device. Its two semi-circular halves were opened wide, looking expectant to have something on which to close. Ricky held out his paw.

"Your *other* paw," Rupert said impatiently.

Ricky quickly held out his left paw and pulled the other back.

"Of course," Ricky said with an uneasy laugh. It's funny how even the most basic things seem difficult when you are about to risk your life in a contraption that may or may not be functioning properly.

Rupert clicked the wristband together and Ricky rubbed the cold metal to warm it up a bit. He and it would be spending a lot of time together.

"So… what do you think happened to the first two travelers?" Ricky asked with morbid curiosity.

Rupert gave Ricky a disapproving look with an arched eyebrow. "They were sent to exactly the time and place they were supposed to."

"But then why didn't it work? Why were they never heard from again?" Ricky asked.

"Yes, I'm ready," he said with conviction, his eyes bright.

There was a loud tone that filled the room and the red circle was now fully closed. It started to pulse and flash in a steady rhythm. Rupert was grinning and moved closer to a large glowing display. He looked up at Ricky for a moment, and then dramatically smacked a large round button.

A series of thuds and clicks seemed to come from everywhere. That faint humming sound from before was now increasing in volume and intensity. Ricky could feel the room vibrating. It made his fur tickle.

The door of the chamber closed automatically and sealed itself with a motorized whir and a hiss of air.

"Oh, before you go," Rupert said quickly, his voice now being amplified somehow within the chamber. "There is another interesting aspect of time travel that real time travelers have to be prepared for – that is, it's not an instantaneous process."

Ricky was suddenly curious why no one had mentioned this sooner. "What do you mean?" he asked hurriedly.

"To an outside observer it might seem to happen pretty quickly, but for the time traveler themselves, it takes a bit of time," Rupert said. His voice was loud in the chamber at first but getting quieter now. "Roughly a minute or so as the transfer solidifies. During that time, the traveler's origin world starts to disappear while the destination emerges into existence..."

Rupert's voice was starting to fade out. In fact, the entire room was starting to fade out. It was almost like fainting or falling asleep. Ricky had to make sure to keep breathing and not panic.

The dim lights in the chamber were glowing brightly now and everything was getting blurry. The lab was starting to disappear.

In its place, Ricky started to see blue sky.

Then some white fluffy clouds. Then lots of trees. Beautiful, fine trees of all different kinds.

There was a brook too, with flowing water spilling over the rocks in small waterfalls.

Overall it was a pretty lush landscape – like something you would see in those priceless paintings by Bob Ross in the archives.

It was beautiful, peaceful, and he was suddenly filled with hope for the success of his mission. It was working! He was really doing it!

As the scents of foliage from the new timeframe started to fill his nose and he again looked at the trees, his take on the scene took a bit of a dark turn.

There was one problem that was becoming clear; a little detail that he would have to bring up with Rupert if he should ever see him again.

Yes, the trees were lovely, but it occurred to Ricky that he shouldn't be looking down at the tops of them.

"Oh, crumbs," he said softly as gravity took over and he started to fall rapidly towards the quickly expanding ground below him.

CHAPTER TWO: *EMMA*

May 24th, 2019
Connecticut, USA

Completely unaware that her life was about to change rather dramatically due to the time traveling raccoon that was currently arriving near her house, Emma was having a relatively ordinary day.

High school wasn't quite what she expected. Every day for years she had handed in her homework, paid attention to the topic at hand, and in general did what she was supposed to do. It was boring and terrifying all at once, and that was something you were just supposed to accept and get used to.

Lately she found herself getting a little more distracted. She was doodling an intricate picture of a tree on her notebook cover when she noticed that her English teacher, Mr. Beckwith was looking at her expectedly. He had scruffy blonde hair and two pens clipped to his plaid button-down shirt pocket. One black, one red.

"Miss Gregor, would you like to explain to the rest of the class what Mark Twain meant in that quote?"

"Um, sure. Which part?" she asked. There was a collection of giggles from the rest of the class who must have heard exactly which part already.

He read it back again. *"Courage is resistance to fear, mastery of fear, not absence of fear."*

It was a fitting quote given that she intensely disliked speaking out in class.

"Well, I think that Mr. Twain was saying that courage is different than we might think," she said cautiously.

Mr. Beckwith teasingly prodded her to elaborate. "Oh yeah? How so?" he asked as he leaned back on his desk as if he knew she would give the correct answer. He liked to call on her when the rest of the class didn't seem to get something.

"Um, well, we think of courageous people as those who have no fear and bravely face any challenge without a second thought."

"And that's not the case? If they aren't brave, then what are they?"

Emma wasn't sure how pointed to be in her answer, but she risked being blunt.

"They are fools." More giggles from the class, but the teacher smiled.

"Ok, so if those people are fools, then who are the brave ones?"

Emma smiled a little in return. "The truly courageous ones are those who *do* feel fear but act anyway. It burns them up inside and tortures their mind with doubt, but they press on if the cause is just. Those who are *most* afraid are the most courageous."

Her teacher grinned and seemed impressed with her answer, but her classmates must have felt out-gunned and shot her somewhat hostile glances. She was suddenly glad the class was almost over.

Mr. Beckwith was one of her favorite teachers. He genuinely cared and wanted to help all of his students. But he was also the teacher who had told Emma's dad that she was "painfully shy" at times and it was limiting her potential. So she was trying to work on that, but it was a bit of a struggle.

It had been rough since Mom died.

Her therapist had said it was "social anxiety mixed with grief". Some of the boys in her class summed it up more concisely. What was the exact term they used? Oh yeah, *weird*. That was it. Just what a teenage girl wants to hear!

Later in the day, while daydreaming in her Social Studies class she mused about her dating prospects and briefly considered joining a convent to become a nun. Not that she was big on religion, but at least the pressure would be off. No one harasses a penguin. Or at least if they do, there is the pretty hefty threat of eternal damnation for doing so. There were perks.

The rest of the day continued in a similar fashion. Lunch was pretty uneventful. As usual, she sat alone towards the back of the cafeteria. It was easier that way.

A few minutes after she sat down, a group of three girls came over and were about to sit down on the other end of the table. That is, until they saw that Emma was already there. Their trays narrowly missed touching the tabletop as they lifted them back up and swerved towards another table.

"Sorry, didn't see that this one was taken," one of them said. Emma guessed it was nice that she said anything at all.

On some days a few of her braver classmates would actually sit with her and try to strike up a conversation, but evidently there is only so much awkward silence they could take. No one made the attempt today.

At least it was Friday, so that meant pepperoni pizza. Southern Connecticut is known for some of the best pizza in the country, but unfortunately this was decidedly *not* that kind of pizza. Emma wasn't sure where it came from, but she was pretty sure it wasn't Wooster Street in New Haven. Anything made in bulk and delivered as frozen bricks on a truck to be re-heated by cafeteria workers wasn't likely to be anything special. But that being said, it's still pizza, and better than some of the other questionable options they serve the rest of the week.

Emma laughed to herself as she thought about the foods they served. The most common mystery meat was what she dubbed "chorkish" – the chameleon of cafeteria foods. It was a round, breaded patty of unknown origin and nondescript taste. It had no smell whatsoever.

If it was served on a bun, they called it chicken. Served on a plate with gravy it was pork. Replace the gravy with tartar sauce, and voila! Fish. Who knows what animal it really came from, but its amazing versatility is what earned it the multipurpose name.

So in this light, the pepperoni pizza was a welcome treat. They always served it with a bit of salad on the side splashed with some watery Italian dressing. That made it seem like the school was trying to balance things out a little. I see something green on the plate! It must be healthy. Good job, school.

In biology class it was frog dissection day. Emma didn't think it was particularly useful, but it was much easier to just go along with it. She pried at her splayed frog a bit, wondering what kind of life it might have had if it weren't raised in captivity and delivered to her classroom in a plastic bag.

"Emma, dissecting a frog doesn't mean simply poking at it with your forceps," Mrs. Bombach said sternly with a disapproving look.

"Yes, Ma'am," Emma replied. Mrs. Bombach was definitely *not* one of her favorite teachers. It was a shame too, since Emma really loved science. A bad teacher can really squash any enthusiasm for a subject pretty quickly.

She glanced at the lab printout to see what area to focus on next and proceeded to cut with the scalpel. But it wasn't long before she was thinking about the potential life of the frog again.

Maybe it would have lived in a little pond in the woods. Maybe it would have chirped with joy at this time of year when the weather starts getting warm. Near her house there was a pond that she and her mom called "Peeper Pond" and on warm nights the sound was so loud it was almost deafening.

Evidently, attracting a mate is pretty important to frogs, and they get all crazy and shout about it when the mood strikes. Humans pretty much do that too, so it made sense.

While Emma was daydreaming about the frog and wondering what sort of housing options there were for hard-working amphibians, her lab partner, Billy, was playing around with one of the frog's eyeballs and showing it off to his friend across the room. Emma tried to block out the conversation but having Billy right in her ear made that pretty difficult.

"They bounce! Hey man, you gotta try this. Yeah, just pop it out with that metal tool. I know, right?!" Billy was very proud of his discovery.

This brief interaction earned another stern look from the teacher that made Billy take it down a notch. The world may never know how close Billy was to some world-changing revelation about the elasticity and bounciness of this particular frog's eyeball. A missed opportunity for sure.

Billy seemed a little bummed and asked for about the fifth time, "So, what are we supposed to do with this frog?"

Emma was pretty convinced that group work was punishment for all of the good students of the world. The "curse of competence" her mom used to call it. So, you're a good student? Great. Here's your lab partner. See if you can do something with him.

Apart from hating group projects, Emma wasn't sure exactly why this lesson was so necessary in this day and age anyway. After all, there were lots of videos of other people doing frog dissections. They could just watch one. Heck, they could watch it three times over just in the time it took to setup their lab stations.

There were also virtual apps that let you take the frog apart and put it back together in 3D augmented reality. She had seen some of them, and it was actually a lot easier to see what the different parts were on that app than it was in real life. The organs had labels and were animated to show how they worked.

So, what was the point of these dozen or so frogs being bred in captivity, killed, and delivered to their class? Maybe Billy was on to something – the one thing the app couldn't replicate was the feel of cutting apart a once living creature. Well, that and the smell. It was pretty unique.

Emma cut a little further into Herbert - since he had made the ultimate sacrifice, he at least deserved a name - and found his tiny frog heart as instructed. Then they moved down and checked out the liver. Man, this thing had a huge liver! Emma mused that Herbert must have been able to drink his friends under the table at the local frog pub.

As interesting as Herbert's huge liver was though, Emma thought that it still seemed like a disproportional sacrifice for a very small benefit. The problem was that the sacrifice was being made by the frogs, who didn't have much of a say in the matter. The benefit is ostensibly for her and her classmates, but Emma had a feeling the only people who were really benefiting here were the frog breeders. It was also strange to think that was a possible career option.

When her guidance counselor asked what she wanted to do with her professional life, she might have to say "frog breeder" just to see her reaction. What colleges should she shortlist, and what SAT score should she shoot for to make that dream come true? Did she think she would have a chance at Yale?

Even though Emma felt this was a colossal waste of both frog life and her time, it wasn't worth making a fuss over. What could she do? Complain to the teacher? Stand up on the desk and liberate the frogs out of the window?

Her dad had showed her the movie "E.T." once and she recalled the scene where the kid went off the deep end because of some alien, and they had a frog revolution in the classroom. They tossed them out of the window, and they hopped away to a better life. Frog justice at last!

But her frog was already dead. She guessed that the school system learned their lesson in a post-E.T. world and took that possibility out of the mix. Dead frogs in bags don't inspire thoughts of rebellion quite the same way.

The bell finally rang, and everyone quickly cleaned up their workstations. As Emma put their pins and tools into a metal tray, she saw the teacher rolling out a large cart of fresh frogs for the next class.

And what of Herbert? He was destined for the large trashcan by the door, along with all of his nameless compatriots. Billy and his friend tried to see how far away they could get from the can and still score a point with the friend's frog. Decidedly more serious, Emma quietly said "thanks" as she tossed Herbert into the bin. He slid along the plastic liner and made a small thump at the bottom.

She made her way to the final class of the day, a study hall. She quickly did her remaining homework, which left her with some time to think. More accurately, to overthink. It was one of her strongest skills, actually. It's obvious why people do things that make them feel good – sex, drugs, rock 'n' roll – that all makes sense. But those who can overthink things and make themselves miserable with repeated results should probably be eligible for some kind of award or something. At least Emma thought so.

In a way she was jealous of Billy the eyeball bouncer – he seemed pretty carefree. Being sensitive made her miserable sometimes and she often wished she could just let things go. Her mom used to say that was one of the things she loved most about Emma and what made her unique. But Herbert was gone and so was Mom. Ugh.

Some people say your teenage years are supposed to be amazing and the best of your life, but Emma had a feeling hers were filled with too many thoughts like these. Maybe things would lighten up once she got a job and a mortgage.

The final bell of the day saved her from any deeper musings, and she packed up her things. She threaded her way through crowded and noisy halls to get to the front doors. What were all of these kids talking about? What was important to other teenagers? It was a mix of "he said / she said", plans for the weekend, complaints about the smell coming from the bio lab, and various idle chitchat.

Emma longed for something a bit more solid. Something that *means* something. Her dad had said that college is usually the place for that, but should she just wait until then? Should she just create a file cabinet full of folders on various subjects and accumulate any advanced thoughts until someone else was ready to discuss them? She had always felt more comfortable with adults than others her own age. Animals too. They were good listeners even if they didn't know what the heck you were babbling about.

Students poured out of the brick school building and piled into yellow buses and various SUVs and minivans. Emma lived only a few miles away from the school and the weather was nice, so she had ridden her bike in. She undid the padlock keeping her bike attached to the bike rack and hopped on with a little bounce.

Riding her bike was definitely a highlight of her day. The wind in her long brown hair, the rush of acceleration down the hills and the sense of accomplishment cresting the next hill. Flowering trees lined the roads and the warm breeze wicked away a bit of sweat. Squirrels chased each other in the trees, and birds fluttered from branch to branch while singing sweet songs. It was primal in a way, and maybe a bit silly, but she liked it all the same.

"Enjoy life when you can," her therapist had said. Try not to get caught up in so much deep thought. Breathe better. Sleep better. Eat better. Get some (real) friends. All excellent suggestions. But like any form of self-improvement it sometimes seemed like too much work. Riding her bike didn't feel like work. It was, dare she say it, fun!

There was usually some part of her brain that liked to pipe up when she was having fun. It is the voice in your head that sensitive people know well.

Having fun are you? Great! But don't forget you have that thing to do later. Yeah, that's gonna suck. Oh yeah, and don't forget that comment that kid next to you made in math class. We'll need to obsess over that for a while. And don't forget your mom is dead. Don't forget life is going to get a lot harder from here on out.

Get the idea? Yeah, it's a bit of a bummer. It's like Gollum from *The Lord of the Rings* taking up permanent residence in your head. But the inner naysayer that is the Brain Gollum seems to have a weakness for a bike ride. Maybe it's because the survival part of your brain takes over to make sure you don't become a permanent fixture on a telephone pole or car hood. No matter why it happened, Emma was glad for it and enjoyed the ride.

The beautiful warm weather helped too. Everything seems so much nicer when there is a warm breeze on your face. Is this how the people in Hawaii feel all the time? The world will be ok. Everything's ok.

Emma was enjoying her ride so much she almost forgot to stop at Al and Bob's butcher shop. She was supposed to pick up the burgers that would be central to this weekend's barbecue plans with her dad. Her dad had ordered and paid for them in advance, so she just had to grab them on her way home.

She liked going to the shop – it was nicely decorated with tile and wood, smelled of delicious cooking food, and the butchers, Al and Bob were quite a pair. Al was a portly middle-aged man who was perpetually smiling and would always ask about your family or what you had going on that week. Unlike some other people, he seemed genuinely interested in the answers. He made you feel special, even if it was only for a quick 5-minute conversation while he was wrapping up your order. Emma liked him a lot and was glad for the chance to see him today.

She parked her bike and then thought about the other half of the shop's ownership – Bob. Bob was lanky and less overtly cheery, but served as a nice counterpoint to Al. Bob was the sarcastic and surly curmudgeon. He was also really nice once you got beyond the gruff exterior. While Al was up front and worked the counter, Bob worked more in the back. You could often hear him swearing at whatever box he was opening or bantering back and forth with Al when he would ask for something. Emma was glad that today was no different.

As she walked into the store, she admired the stocked shelves of breads, spices, pastas, and snacks. The scent of cooking meats and spices hung thick in the air. She admired the refrigerated counter area with the glass front that let you see all of the options and point out your meat of choice. Everything was very clean, tidy, and bright. A well-kept shop is a treasure in a chaotic world.

Al was whistling while wiping down the counter when he spotted Emma. His face lit up right away.

"Hey there, Emma! Great to see you. How has your day been so far?" he asked as he folded up the towel and focused all of his attention on her.

Emma thought for a moment that maybe she could tell him about her actual day, Herbert and all, but then thought better of it. People often ask about your day, but they seldom really want to know the details. Al was the kind of person that would actually listen intently and probably then offer sage advice, but she didn't think she wanted to burden him with that kind of time-consuming endeavor right now.

"Oh, fine. Everything's fine. Just another day in paradise," she quipped.

"Yes, yes, it is!" Al said in agreement with her statement. Emma couldn't tell if he was being serious or not. Probably was. Lucky guy.

She reminded him that her dad should have called in the order, and he found the details on a small pad he had on the counter behind him. He called it out to Bob like a waiter calls out an order to a chef in one of those super busy restaurants you see on TV shows.

Bob was fussing with something in the back so Emma couldn't see him, but she heard his distinctively crabby voice "You want how many burgers? Good God, they might as well go to the farm and get the whole cow to save us some trouble!"

Al rolled his eyes, turned his head and yelled back, "It's for Emma, you putz! Be nice. And besides, if she went to the farm for an entire cow we'd be out of business."

Bob poked his head out of the freezer door and said a bit too loud, "Hi Emma! Sorry love, just messin' with ya."

"No worries," replied Emma. "Your burgers are good but it's the sarcasm that keeps me coming back." At this, Bob smiled broadly and disappeared back into the freezer.

A moment later, he barked "Order up!" and Emma saw a large chunk of meat fly out of the back to the expectant hands of Al. Emma mused they should have their own circus act with meat flinging skills like this.

Al held the large red and white marbled chunk up in the air. "I'll get this freshly ground up for you and have you ready to go in just a jiffy. Big party this weekend?"

Emma wasn't really looking forward to the people coming over but didn't want to say that out loud. "Yup. My dad is hosting a Memorial Day picnic for some of his friends." At least there would be lots of good food to enjoy and she could probably just grab a plateful and run off into the woods to go sit by the brook to eat in peace.

After being gone for a few minutes, Al returned with a large, bright white parcel in his hand that he sealed with yellow tape and wrote on with a black marker. "Here ya go, Emma, you're all set. Did you want that to go or shall I get you a plate and fork?"

Emma had heard the joke many times before but still found it funny and giggled.

"Not today, but thanks."

Al laughed. "Should be delicious – I know you'll enjoy it. Send my best to your dad," he said as he beamed one of his infectious (and possibly trademarked) smiles.

"Will do, Al. Thank you," she smiled back. She took the heavy parcel and popped it into an insulated bag in her backpack.

On the way out she heard Bob screaming from the back again. "…damn trash pandas got into the dumpster, *again!* How the hell did they do that? I've tried bungees cords, ropes, and even chains, and they still get in there."

"They're mocking you, Bob," Al said with a chuckle. He seemed much more amused at this news than Bob did. "It's not like it matters if the raccoons eat what we've thrown out anyway."

Bob definitely didn't agree with that. "They're furry stomachs with legs is what they are. Villains in masks. And they make a huge mess! It's like they had an all-night meat bender back here. It's even on the walls! What the… where's the duct tape?!"

Al and Emma looked at each other with an equal sense of levity about this and both had to stifle any laughs that Bob would hear.

Suddenly there was some kind of loud *splat* sound that came from the back of the store, and they heard Bob cry out "For God's sake!" At this, Al finally laughed out loud and Emma raised her hands to her mouth as she cracked up and let out a snort.

"You had better go now, this might get ugly," Al warned. She saw a blur through the back door that she assumed was Bob. The blur had a mop and bucket, as well as a command of curse words she found quite impressive.

Taking Al's advice, she headed out of the front door and said goodbye with a sheepish grin and a wave.

Was it wrong to reap the benefits of humor from someone else's misery? Probably. But life is like that. You have to enjoy it when you can.

CHAPTER THREE: *MONIQUE*

When Ricky came to, he recalled a quick flash of the fall out of the sky and was pretty sure he was dead. He was looking up at a beautiful face of another raccoon, one that smiled when she saw he was waking up.

"Try not to move too much. Your leg is pretty well broken," she said.

Ricky groggily glanced down and saw that a bandage was wrapped around the full length of his left leg. The white wrapping was a stark contrast to his reddish-brown fur. There was a dull bit of pain, but not anywhere near what he would expect for a freshly broken leg. Not dead, that was good. But injured – that's going to be a big problem for the mission.

"Did you bind my leg?" he asked groggily.

She looked over at the dressing and seemed to shrink humbly. "Oh, heavens no! The doc from down the street did that. Gave you twelve stitches and something for the pain too, so you might feel a little woozy."

Without looking, Ricky did a quick check with his paw to make sure his wristband was still on his left wrist. It was, thank goodness.

"What is your name?" Ricky asked, feeling the wooziness she spoke of. "What happened while I was out?"

"I'm Monique," she said with a happy bit of chattering sound, as if she was flattered that he would ask what her name was. "And you?"

"Ricky," he said weakly.

"Well, nice to meet you, Ricky. I was walking along the brook having a lovely day, cooling off my paws in the nice running water, when all of sudden you came crashing down next to me."

She played with her gray-brown and black striped tail a little as she continued. "You must have been really way up in one of those tall oak trees, because you hit with such a noise, I thought you might have been killed. Fortunately, you landed in a softer muddy area right next to the brook, which probably saved you."

She looked down at his leg. "Well, most of you anyway. Your leg hit one of those large stones that line the edges of the brook, and, well, you know what that did. It took quite a bit of cleaning to get all of the blood and mud off of you."

Realizing someone must have sponged all of that off of his fur, Ricky suddenly felt a bit embarrassed, but tried to stay focused. He still had lots of questions. "And then you brought me to your doctor friend?"

Monique laughed. "I wouldn't say the vet is my friend per se, though she is very nice. And I didn't bring you myself, I had to get help for that."

"Vet?" Ricky asked.

"Sure, veterinarian. A human that works as an animal doctor," Monique said as she began rummaging around for something.

Ricky had been trained for this mission, albeit in a rushed fashion. His fall and injury must have rattled his brain a little. Humans and animals in this time had very strange relationships with each other. Very strange, indeed. In fact, that was the main reason for the entire…

"Ow!" Ricky exclaimed. He had tried to sit up and wasn't expecting the shooting pain that went up his leg to his back.

"Easy now," Monique said soothingly. She helped him sit up as Ricky grimaced through the pain and got a better look at the surroundings. They were both in a small building that looked like a wooden shed. It had rakes and shovels on the walls, and a bunch of pieces of wood and white wallboards stacked up on one side. It smelled of sweet pine. His keen ears picked up the songs of a few birds singing outside.

Once Monique was sure that he was stable enough to sit upright on his own, she handed Ricky some water to drink. He enjoyed the sweet cooling liquid and squished the flexible semi-transparent cup in his paws as he looked it over.

"Plastic?" he asked.

Monique looked at the cup and then back at Ricky with puzzlement. "Of course."

Ricky chuckled a little and again tried to stay focused on the task at hand. "So, this human veterinarian, who is not a friend, is the one who patched me up, but you needed help to get me to her?"

Monique smiled gently. "You must have really hit your head hard. Yes, of course. I can't just walk up to the humans and tell them what I want; it's never that easy."

"Because they don't understand you?" Ricky asked.

"Of course not," she said with a laugh. "Wouldn't things be easier if they did!" she said as she sighed longingly at such an absurd notion.

"I went to the humans who live in the house," she said as she pointed out of one of the small windows in the shed towards a larger building. "Emma is the young human girl who lives there with her father."

She smiled and puffed up her fur a little with what looked like pride. "Humans in general are not to be trusted, but these two are different."

"Different?" Ricky asked.

"Yes, they regularly give us locals a variety of food, water, and even take us to the vet when we get sick or injured."

"But you don't talk to her?" Ricky asked, still trying to clarify their relationship.

"She talks to me a lot and I love to listen, but she never understands what I say to her, of course."

Monique took Ricky's empty cup and put it down on a nearby crate. She ran her paw along the dark wood tenderly.

"Thanks to her, this is my home," she said. She then turned and pointed to the far end of the shed. "Emma put in a small flappy door in the wall over there so that I can stay here and come and go as I please."

She then gestured towards the other corners. "There is also a heated pad for a bed and that white cube thing over there has snacks."

Ricky perked up at the mention of snacks. He felt like he was starving but was still puzzled and needed some answers. "So, if she can't understand you, how did you get this girl…"

"Emma," Monique offered politely.

"Yes, Emma," Ricky continued. "How did you get Emma to bring me to the vet?"

Monique seemed a little embarrassed, but said "Well, let's just say it involved a lot of scratching at the front door, scratching at the back door, and me trying to yell at her that this was an emergency and I needed her help right away."

"And that worked?" Ricky asked.

"Well, at first, she must have thought I was hungry or something because she kept giving me cookies. I got a little distracted and ate them of course."

"Of course," Ricky echoed.

"But when I didn't stop yelling afterward, she came back with some grapes. When that didn't work…"

"Wait, they have grapes?" Ricky asked eagerly.

"Yes, and cookies. I told you these humans are different. I'll get you some," she said as she walked over to the white cube and pulled out a few containers.

"Anyway, Emma finally got the hint that something was up and started to follow me as I was walking away. Then she looked down into the ravine and saw you next to the brook."

Monique pried at the clear containers and removed the flat lids. She handed them to Ricky for him to hold while she pulled out the contents.

"Plastic?" Ricky asked while inspecting them.

Monique looked confused again. "Um, Yes," she said with a puzzled look on her furry face. "Anyway, Emma was very concerned about you, called the vet from down the street, and gave me some more cookies."

"I see," Ricky said.

"Emma told me I was a good girl and also called me 'Lassie' for some reason, which is weird since she's the one that named me Monique."

Ricky didn't know why her name would change, but at least his rescue was becoming clearer.

"So, once the vet patched you up, we brought you back here to rest and recover. Emma setup this additional bed here for you, and she will be stopping by periodically to check on you."

She was holding out one of the plastic containers and Ricky could see a pile of round black and white cookies in it.

He carefully took one and gave it a cautious chew. After a moment his face lit up. "Oh my gosh, this is good!" It had a crunchy outside with a creamy middle that was just divine.

Monique looked pleased. "I know, right? I told you, Emma is the real deal." Ricky wasn't sure he knew exactly what she meant by that phrase, but he seemed to get the general idea.

While crunching away on his second cookie, Ricky looked down at his leg and thought about his mission. It was imperative that he be able to reach his three targets at very specific times. There was no room for error. He might need continued help to do that.

"Do you trust her?" Ricky asked.

"You mean Emma? Absolutely," Monique said. Her face was unwavering.

"Good," Ricky said. "Because I might need more of her help to complete my mission. And yours, if you're willing."

Monique paused for a moment. "Mission?"

Ricky knew that normally he wasn't supposed to share any details of his mission with anyone else but being able to actually complete that mission took priority. "Yes, I'm not just here passing through, I'm here for a reason."

"Ok, well, what *is* your mission, exactly, and who sent you? Are you here from a neighboring town to scope out possible mates or something?" she asked brightly.

"No, nothing like that," Ricky said as he smiled and blushed a bit at the thought. He couldn't be sure, but he thought Monique looked a little disappointed for a moment.

He was about to divulge some of his actual mission details when they heard approaching footsteps getting louder. A moment later, the door of the shed opened up, letting in brilliant sunlight and a slight breeze. A young girl with bright green eyes slowly peered around the edge of the door.

"That's Emma," Monique said with a hushed voice and a smile.

Ricky prepared himself for what needed to happen next.

CHAPTER FOUR: *THE MISSION*

"Ah, you're awake! I was hoping you would be," Emma said quietly as she stepped into the shed and closed the door behind her gently. "I also hoped that you wouldn't freak out in here and try to claw your way out or something. Or attack my friend Monique here. After all it was her that led me to you." She took another step cautiously towards Ricky.

"I know, I'm quite grateful," Ricky said, giving Monique a thankful look.

"AAAAHH!" Emma screamed as she nearly jumped out of her skin and fell backwards as her eyes went wide.

"What? What did I say?" Ricky said holding his paws up in the air. He wasn't sure why this girl had gone from calm to crazed in such a short amount of time. Did he offend her somehow?

Emma was keeping her distance and looking around at the edges of the shed. "Dad? Are you doing this somehow with a wireless speaker or something?!" she asked of the walls. "You're hilarious. I know you're still trying to get me back for wrapping every item in your office in bubble wrap on April Fool's day, but this is just weird."

Ricky had no idea what she was talking about. "Look, I just wanted to say thank you for saving me and getting my leg patched up."

Emma's head snapped back in Ricky's direction. Her eyes were now laser focused on his mouth and face. "Say that again."

Ricky looked at Monique curiously, and Monique looked almost as surprised as Emma. Her mouth was wide open, and her long whiskers were twitching slightly.

What was going on? Ricky turned back to Emma and repeated very slowly, "I said… I want to thank you for saving me and getting my leg patched up. Without you I might have been a goner."

Emma was moving closer and closer as Ricky was talking, and for some reason looked like she had either seen a ghost or was about to wrestle a cobra.

He still wasn't sure what to make of all of this, so he continued. "My name is Ricky, and it's nice to meet you," he said as he gave a little wave with his paw. "I'm on a very important mission, and without you saving me, I don't know what would have happened."

Emma stared at him in disbelief.

"Why are you both being so weird right now?" Ricky asked as he turned to look back at Monique in hope of some answers.

Monique had a confused look on her furry face. "Ricky, how in the world can she understand you?" she asked in almost a whisper.

Monique then explained again how she and the other animals could always understand Emma and the other humans, but that the humans could never understand them.

She went on further to explain that it is a universal guideline among the animals that the humans are generally dangerous and not to be trusted. Anyone who does trust them too much would be putting their own lives at risk, so it is always best to keep it quiet that the animals actually know a lot more than they are letting on.

Emma saw the two raccoons looking at each other and heard Monique making some normal raccoon sounds – complicated chittering, a few purrs, and a spattering of chirps. Ricky would nod and interject with the occasional response. "Ok," "yeah, I guess that makes sense," "no," "uh-huh," etc.

After a few moments, Ricky turned back to Emma. "You

didn't catch any of that?" he asked.

"Nope. Just your side. Why can you talk? How can a raccoon possibly speak English?!" Emma was looking flabbergasted but also had a bit of a grin that was creeping onto her face. She was getting closer again.

Ricky paused for a moment and looked at his wristband. He pawed at it a bit and his thoughts started to form a little better. During training they had told him something like this might happen. It was just really strange to actually have it happen in real life.

Emma saw him pawing at the wristband. "Is that a translator or something? The vet and I couldn't get it off of you, so we figured it was a wildlife tracking device or something."

Ricky made a complicated motion with his paw around the edges of the wristband and it released with a spring-like snap. He took it off of his wrist, rubbed the fur underneath a bit, and then asked Monique to hold out her paw. Reluctantly she held out her arm and Ricky closed the wristband around her with a solid click. "Now say something to Emma."

Monique looked inquisitively down at the wristband and slowly lifted her masked face back up to look at Emma.

"Hi."

"AAHH! Oh my God that's amazing!" Emma was giddily laughing this time and came in close to inspect both Monique and the wristband while kneeling. "How does it work?" Emma's mouth was wide open as she rotated Monique's arm to examine every facet of the wondrous device. Monique was grinning cheerfully.

Ricky was about to start explaining when he realized she wouldn't understand him until he had it back. Monique caught on too and held her wrist out back in Rick's direction. He made the switch and continued.

"I don't know all of the science behind it, but the general premise is that it actively analyzes the brain waves and natural speech patterns of the wearer. It then takes that information and projects a translation of it directly to any listener within a small radius."

Emma wasn't bothering to hide her amazement. "I had no idea this kind of technology existed!"

"Well, it's funny that you should say that… because technically it doesn't. At least not… *yet*," Ricky said cautiously.

Emma was squinting her eyes pensively. "So, it's from… the future?"

"Yes, and so am I in fact," he said with as much earnestness as he could muster. Ricky had decided he might as well go all in. There was no other way that he could complete his mission in his current state without her help.

Emma was still processing but seemed to be taking it all pretty well. "Normally I would be incredibly skeptical of anyone saying something that outlandish, but then again, when a talking raccoon tells you why they can talk, it's surprisingly convincing."

She looked over at Monique who was scrunching up her shoulders and nodding in agreement. Emma's face lit up as she laughed a little at the craziness of it all, but Ricky saw something else in her expression as well. Was it relief? Hope? He wasn't sure.

Almost forgetting the task at hand, he had to remind himself to stay focused. "I know it's a lot to take in, but it's true. I've been sent from the future on a mission of the upmost importance."

Emma was hooked. "What is your mission? Tell me how I can help," she said sincerely.

Ricky's relief was almost palpable. He took a big breath and exhaled slowly. "Ok, there's not a lot of time for details, but here's the short version. The world that I left - your future - is a very different place from what you know now."

"What year are you from? How far back have you come? What is it like? Are there flying cars?" Emma's head was filled with questions!

Ricky paused for a moment. "Well, I'm not supposed to give too many specific details, but what I can say is that I'm coming from a pretty long way off. A lot has happened between our times, and a great deal of it is not good." His face turned a bit somber at this, and Emma noticed.

"Like, how not good?" Emma asked. "Are the humans in your time at war or something? We always seem to be doing stupid things like that."

"That's just it," Ricky continued. "There *aren't* any humans in my time. None. They have all died out, and it wasn't a pleasant process. You are the first human I've ever seen in real life."

Emma always assumed that humans would be the cause of their own demise and even thought it would be a good thing for the planet at times. So, she was surprised when she found herself hit with a wave of sadness at hearing it actually happened. Past tense.

"Wow. How did it happen?" she asked as she brushed a few strands of her brown hair away from her eyes and over her ear. She had a thoughtful look on her face.

Ricky answered gently, realizing this might be difficult for her to hear. "It was actually a number of things over a long period of time. Yes, there was war among the humans, but the most devastating blows came from famine and disease caused by shifts in the global climate."

"That makes some sense," Emma said. "Not a day goes by that you don't hear some bickering about 'global warming' or 'climate change' on the news or online."

Ricky's eyes went wide. "So, you *do* know what's happening? We were never sure how much the humans of your time knew about what was going on. What have you heard? Why isn't anyone doing something about it?"

Emma saw the concern in his furry face and looked slightly embarrassed. "Well, practically every scientist agrees that humans are causing serious problems for the planet. Burning fossil fuels, reproducing like crazy, dumping waste wherever we can, and just generally being terrible stewards of the only planet we have."

Ricky looked perplexed. "So why aren't you *doing* anything

about it? The fate of your entire species is at stake!"

"Well, there are others who disagree," Emma said with noticeable frustration.

"Other scientists?"

"Maybe some, but generally the opponents aren't even scientists. But they *are* loud about it and I think people listen because it's easier to think that way. People don't like to change."

"How can they not see what's going on? What is their defense?" Ricky asked.

Emma rolled her eyes. "They say a bunch of things. They say that the planet is fine, human activity is too small to affect the entire planet, and any warming we are seeing is just a natural trend that we can't do anything about. It's very tiring to listen to and most people feel pretty helpless about it."

Ricky was shaking his head as if he couldn't comprehend it. "Even if some humans don't think that climate change is real, why are they still opposed to some of the obviously beneficial things?"

"What do you mean?" Emma asked.

"Well, harnessing the power of the sun through solar collectors means clean and free electricity. Do humans like the smell of burning coal or something? Isn't your country dependent on other countries for oil? Why not break free from that?"

"I don't know," Emma said honestly. "Maybe because people are making money off of the old ways of doing things."

"Maybe," Ricky said.

Emma was looking up at the ceiling as if searching for answers or the right questions to ask. "Regardless of what we are or aren't doing though, how do changes to the climate wipe out all humans? I know warming of the planet can eventually cause flooding from the melting ice caps. But how does that kill *everyone*? I don't get it."

Ricky paused for a moment, trying to think of a relatively quick way to explain what happened. "Well, you are right that as the planet warmed, the polar ice caps that modern humans have always known, started to melt. In your time, most of that ice is currently on land, right?"

"Yes," Emma answered. "Most of it is on top of Greenland and Antarctica."

"Well, that melt water went into the oceans and did indeed raise the global sea level, which directly caused massive floods."

"But that wouldn't be enough to flood the entire world, right?" Emma asked, settling in to sit cross-legged as if back in storytime at primary school.

"You are correct," Ricky said. "It was bad news for anyone on the coastlines, but the inner areas of the continents were safe from that. What they weren't safe from was the secondary effects."

Emma wasn't sure what he meant. "Like what?"

"The fresh water entered the oceans and caused desalination in those areas. Saltwater organisms can't survive in fresh water, so entire ecosystems in the oceans were destroyed."

"Yeah, I guess that would be a bad thing," Emma said.

"On a larger scale, ocean currents were also affected by the cold water disrupting the normal flows. Animal migrations stopped happening. And since all life is interconnected, species started dying off rapidly in a cascade effect."

"Like dominoes?"

"I don't know what dominoes are," Ricky confessed. "But if you mean that one thing causes another to happen, and then even more, then yes."

"Ok, but even if things are bad in the ocean, how does that affect the humans living on land?" Emma asked.

"Soon things really started to spiral out of control," Ricky said. "Once the oceans became unstable, the weather patterns in the atmosphere that farmers depended on became erratic. Crops were lost to sudden cold snaps in the middle of growing seasons. Drought is what hit the humans really hard though."

"That makes sense. You can't grow anything without a steady water supply," Emma agreed.

Ricky was gesturing broadly with his paws. "Large areas of

the planet that used to have regular rains went completely dry. Other areas that were normally dry got the moisture instead. Farmlands became deserts and deserts became muddy flood zones."

Emma was starting to understand the scope of the problem. "I see. I guess we really mucked things up."

But Ricky wasn't done yet. "Unfortunately, There's more. The warming caused increases in insects like mosquitoes and ticks that vectored existing diseases. Malaria alone killed millions. But there was a deadly surprise waiting for the humans as the polar ice melted: emerging infectious diseases."

"What do you mean, like, unknown diseases?" she asked.

"Yes," Ricky said, nodding his head. "Microbes, bacteria, and viruses that the humans had absolutely no resistance to were released en masse from the melting ice. Flooding made them spread even more rapidly."

"But we have hospitals and medicine, couldn't we just treat those that got sick?" Emma asked innocuously.

"The humans scrambled to find treatments and cures, but the economic systems were in tatters. Hospitals were overwhelmed. There were no resources for anything at the scale that would have been needed."

Emma paused for a moment. "So that's it then?"

"I wish that were it," Ricky said. "Things were really bad for the humans, but there was one final blow for all life on earth, and it is due the fact that water is heavy."

Emma blinked her green eyes thoughtfully. "Yeah, of course, but why would that matter?"

"The additional weight of the melt water from the poles moving to other areas of the planet caused greater instability in the crust," Ricky said as he moved his paws around in a circular fashion as if around an invisible ball. "The earth itself was accustomed to the weight distribution being a certain way, and that distribution changed."

"You mean the earth itself started to get squished in different ways?" Emma offered.

"Yeah, that's a good way to put it," Ricky said with a little admiration. "The earth isn't just a solid ball of dirt."

"I learned at the natural history museum that the plates of the earth float on the molten inner layers. That's why we have earthquakes, right?" she asked.

"Yes," Ricky replied. "And earthquakes are tied to tsunamis and volcanoes. Dormant volcanoes and long quiet deep-sea fissures became active – spewing fire, ash, smoke, and even more heat into the atmosphere."

"That's similar to the big extinction event that wiped out the dinosaurs, right?"

"Yes," Ricky said. "Although an asteroid impact played a big role with that. But just like with the dinosaurs, the global temperature flipped when the sun was blocked out almost entirely for years."

"If there's one thing I know from science class, it's that all life on earth depends on the sun," Emma said.

"Yes. Without it, things die very quickly. Adaptable scavengers were the only ones who could eek out an existence during that time. Raccoons included," Ricky said as he looked over at Monique.

"We are definitely an adaptable bunch," Monique said to Ricky with a smile.

"Did any humans survive? Maybe in underground bunkers or something?" Emma asked. She recalled seeing some determined survivalists on a TV show once where they had seemingly prepared for years of underground existence in the event of a nuclear war or something. They had lots of food, water, and something about needing tin foil for hats.

Ricky turned back to face Emma. "For a while there were rumors that maybe some small pockets of humans had survived underground, but we have since determined that to not be possible."

"Are you sure?"

"Yes, my parents were actually archeologists studying humans and the Plastic Age, so I used to go with them sometimes on digs to explore…"

"Wait, the Age of *what*?" Emma asked while holding out her hand in front of her in a stopping gesture. "Did you say the *Plastic Age*?"

"Uh… yes," Ricky said sheepishly.

"I thought this was the *Information Age*, no?" Emma asked with bewilderment.

"Um… heh heh. No," Ricky said with an uneasy laugh. "Archeologists name periods of civilization based on what they find – for example from the Stone Age they would find stone tools. From the Bronze Age they found lots of bronze artifacts, etc."

"Yeah, in the Iron Age they find iron tools, I get it," Emma said, starting to understand.

Ricky continued. "I guess people from this time might have a different perspective, or lack thereof, but from the future looking back, this is the time period where plastic defines what you can create easily and basically covers the planet."

Ricky picked up the plastic water cup from earlier and looked it over in the light. "Whenever we dig and find plastic, we know exactly what time period it's from. And not just large pieces. Tiny bits are in the water, in the air, and in the soil and food chain. Heck, it's even in you!" he said as he pointed to Emma.

Emma instinctively put a hand on her stomach and looked slightly ill at the thought of being filled with plastic particles.

"Anyway," Ricky continued as he put the cup back, "my parents were always fascinated with the long-lost humans and what happened to them. We discovered a number of underground shelters that probably supported life for a few years, but those can only be useful for so long."

"Yeah, I suppose even in the best of shelters you would need to replenish supplies eventually," Emma said.

"Yes, Ricky agreed. "With no way to do that, they were all doomed, albeit at a slower rate than some of those on the surface. Every shelter ever discovered just had dead human remains in them."

Emma looked questioningly at Ricky and he knew her question. "Yes, that's it," he said somberly.

"So, you're here from the future to save humanity?" Emma asked.

"In part," Ricky agreed. "A lot of my mission really relates to the other inhabitants of the world as well – the animals."

"The animals?" Emma asked. "But you survived."

"Well, many of us did survive the extinction event, but it's been a difficult existence and there were so many that were lost. It was decided that if we could change things for the better, that we should."

"Do you know how many were lost?" Emma asked.

"It's a heartbreaking number." Ricky said. "Even now in your time, there are roughly one hundred and fifty to two hundred species of plant, insect, bird, and mammal species that are going extinct *every day*."

"Are you kidding?" Emma asked with unmasked shock on her face. "Things don't even seem that bad yet."

"No, and once things really take a turn it just gets worse and worse. The end result is almost unfathomable."

"Ok, but how can you change something so big?" Emma asked.

"While it's a complicated issue with many factors, our researchers and scholars have been able to pinpoint the causes of the calamities that were, in fact, preventable. And a lot of the changes that need to happen relate to how humans interact with the animals of this world."

"How we interact with animals?"

"Yes," Ricky said. "In hindsight it was easy to see what the problems were that led up to the fall. Humans were the primary cause of their own demise, but their actions towards other life on the planet was devastating. Every animal, every plant, every insect. No one is immune when you are dealing with global actions or inactions."

Emma was nodding her head as if she had assembled all

of the pieces of a huge puzzle and was taking a step back to see it all. "So… by improving relations between humans and animals… you can save humanity and therefore the animals as well?" she asked hoping she had put it all together correctly.

"Yes!" Ricky said, happily. "All life on the planet is interconnected. The hope is that if my mission is successful, much of this misery can be avoided for all."

"But then what happens to the world you left?" Emma asked.

"The world I left behind will no longer exist," Ricky said. "In its place, there will hopefully be a different timeline and planet where humans and animals can live together in peace on a sustainable planet."

"Ok, but, wait…" Emma was still trying to understand how anything Ricky could do might avert such a disaster. "Are you sure this is an unavoidable future? We are recycling a bunch of stuff these days and Dad just got solar panels on the house and an electric car. Doesn't that work?"

Ricky had to contain a bit of frustration. "Every amount helps and it's great that you are doing something in your own lives, but just pockets of recycling or small-scale changes won't do anything significant."

Ricky paused for a moment, trying to think of a way to convey the enormity of the problem. "Do you know how many humans are currently on the planet compared to the past?"

"I'm really not sure," Emma admitted.

Ricky tapped his wristband in a few quick motions. "Your grandparents probably grew up in the 1960s, right?"

Emma had to think for a moment. "Yeah, I guess so. They were into the Beatles and The Doors and all that stuff."

Ricky had no idea what beetles and doorways had to do with the topic at hand but didn't want to get sidetracked. "Well, in 1960 there were about 3 billion humans on this planet. That wasn't that long ago. Want to know how many there are right now?"

"Probably not, but hit me with it," Emma said boldly.

"Almost 8 billion people. In the past 50 years of your timeline, the human population has more than *doubled*."

"Wow," Emma said, trying to grasp what that really meant.

Ricky continued. "That's twice as many people on the same planet. At that scale it doesn't matter if they recycle a bit. Every human is consuming vast amounts of resources, using energy, and creating waste. And it's only getting worse."

"I know that the human population is still increasing, so that definitely won't help," Emma said.

"Yes, as the human population and land use go up, the biodiversity of life on the planet is decreasing rapidly. Put all of this together and you have a planet at the cusp of a mass extinction."

"So, what can we do, apart from shipping half of the population off to another planet or something?" Emma asked, feeling a little hopeless in the face of such a huge problem.

"The entire human population needs to enact sweeping and fundamental changes to even have a chance of making a real difference. And unfortunately, in the timeline I come from, that doesn't happen," Ricky said somberly as he hugged his striped tail.

"So, what *is* your mission, exactly?" Emma asked. "What do you have to do?"

Ricky felt a bit of pride at the role he would play and puffed his fur up a little. "I have three very important targets that I need to intercept."

"Targets?"

"Yes. For each one, I have to locate them and carry out certain actions at very specific times."

"How will that stop all of those future calamities from happening?" Emma asked with uncertainty.

"Honestly... I'm not sure," he said as he let go of his tail. "They don't give us all of the details on purpose. All I know is that the smartest minds in the world and the most capable computers poured over the histories of Earth and all of the data to come up with this very specific plan."

"And if you are successful, then the future will be different?"

"Yes. If I intervene in the lives of these three individuals at very specific moments, the timeline will be altered in such a way that improves the future for all life on the planet."

Emma looked deep in thought. Monique had been listening intently through their conversation, but now joined in. "Who is the first, um, target?" she asked quietly.

Knowing Emma couldn't have understood her, Ricky repeated her query and then answered it. It seemed like the easiest way for the three of them to have a conversation.

He held out his own wrist with the shiny wristband on it. There was a black screen-like area that he tapped with his other paw a few times. Some glowing blue lettering appeared on it. "This is all I have on target number one."

A. SMITH
41.377N, -73.030W
5.25.2019
19:23 HRS
METHOD: NANO-PEN

Emma recognized that the numbers and letters were positioning coordinates and punched them in on her phone. A moment later her face lit up with recognition.

"Hey!" she exclaimed. "I know where that is – that's Al and Bob's shop. And Al's last name is Smith, so that must be him – he's the first target. Are you going to help him with his shop or something?"

Ricky removed a small cylindrical device from the back of his wristband and looked at it carefully. It was made of black textured metal and looked like something that was precision crafted. On the side there was a tiny red button that he pressed, and a small needle extended quickly from one end.

"No," Ricky said. "He's going to die."

PART TWO: THE BUTCHER

CHAPTER FIVE: *THE LESS YOU KNOW*

*E*mma was dumbfounded. "What?! You're going to kill Al?! How could you?"

"No, no, no," Ricky said, realizing that came out very wrong. "I mean he's slated to die – naturally. And I'm here to save him with this nano-pen treatment." He slid the black cylinder back into his wristband where it snapped into place magnetically.

Emma was visibly relieved at this news. "Wow, you really scared me there!" she said with a little laugh. "Al is like the nicest guy ever. The thought of anyone murdering him is just terrible."

"Sorry to scare you," Ricky said earnestly. "It's just the opposite. If you think about it, he is in fact so important to the future of the world that I was sent all the way from the future to save him. Well, him and the two others."

Monique looked back and forth between Emma and Ricky with a confused look.

Ricky turned to her and then back to Emma. "It's quite an honor to be here actually and to meet him! He must be one of the greatest and most precious people in all of human history, and *I* get to save him." His eyes sparkled in the black furry mask of his face at this and he beamed proudly.

Emma started to look very puzzled as well and Ricky noticed. "What... he's not that great?" he asked looking between them.

"Well, he is great, sure," Emma said. "He's certainly very

nice and always friendly, but I don't know about *great,* in a save the world kind of way."

Monique shrugged her shoulders in agreement.

"Well, he must be for some reason," Ricky said. "They wouldn't have sent me all this way to save him for nothing."

He didn't like not having all of the details, but that was the way of things with this time travel program. They kept telling him *the less you know the better off you are.* If he knew too many details, he might hesitate or do something different than what he was supposed to do.

Ricky saw that Emma was having a really hard time reasoning out how this Al person could be so important when he thought he heard a noise from the window. He glanced over but didn't see anything.

"Did anyone else hear that?" he asked of them both.

"Hear what?" Emma asked.

Monique shook her head "no".

"Never mind," he said. "Anyway, that's the first part of the mission. There are two other targets, but there is no point in worrying about those until this first part is complete."

He looked back at his wristband to check the information again. "The exact time is tomorrow at 19:23 hours. Emma, I'll need you to get me to that location just before that time so that I can be ready."

"That's 7:23PM, right?" Emma asked. "The shop closes at 6:30, so everyone else should be gone by then. You can hop in the basket on my bike and we can make it. It's not that far."

"Great!" he said with relief. He rubbed his leg and looked at his new bandage again. "My leg is starting to throb a bit and I'm really tired. So, I think it's best if I rest as much as possible now and we can do this together tomorrow."

Emma and Monique both nodded together.

Just then, Ricky saw both of them looking at him differently. In that moment he felt like this could really work. It felt, *right.* Like this was the right team to do this.

"Thank you both," he said sincerely.

Emma held out her hand and he put his paw in it. She shook it gently up and down. "You're welcome, Ricky. It was really great to meet you. Goodnight, Monique."

Monique gave a little wave with her paw and smiled as Emma walked out of the shed and closed the door behind her. Monique then turned to Ricky and surprised him with a strong hug.

"You're very brave to be doing this," she said with palpable concern. "Most of us don't even go out in the daytime for fear of the humans. You will have to be extremely careful." She released him slowly, but her face remained serious.

"I will," he replied. "I'm ready for this."

He believed that, but something in Monique's expression told him he might not be as prepared as he thought.

CHAPTER SIX: *MINKA*

*L*ater that night, Ricky awoke to the proximity alarm on his wristband giving a slight squeeze to alert him to someone approaching. Monique was sound asleep in the bedding nearby, so the source of the alert was definitely not from her.

He strained his eyes to try to make out the small flappy door on the other side of the shed, but it was too dark. A moment later he was surprised to hear a voice talking to him from behind. He whipped his head around in the new direction.

"The humans aren't what you think they are," the voice said quietly.

Ricky was half-awake and couldn't focus his eyes well, but he started to make out a dark form with large yellow eyes peering at him from out of the blackness of the night.

"Who are you? What do you mean?" he managed to say.

"I heard your sad story. Touching and all that you want to save the world. But the humans don't like change. I don't like change either. In fact, I'm perfectly happy with how things are right now." As the voice said this, it came closer.

It sounded silky and vaguely female. Finally, a sliver of moonlight from the window illuminated the face of a cat that was moving closer. The face was almost all black, but with a bit of white fur under the nose and chin. The white extended down the belly, and there were white paws at the end of long black legs. A tuxedo shorthair from the looks of it.

"Who are you and what do you want?" Ricky asked, feeling

a little unsettled.

"I'm Minka. And I don't *want* anything, other than to keep things as they are. I have a good life here and now, and I'm not sure I like the thought of you shaking things up with my humans."

"I'm not here to cause any trouble for you or Emma. I'm actually here to help improve things for everyone," he said.

Minka wasn't convinced. "Well, we'll see about that. I'll stop back tomorrow night after your visit to the shop. Good luck with that."

And just like that – she was gone.

Ricky knew a number of cats from his own time, and while some of them were agreeable and friendly, he also knew that some could be more standoffish. But one universal aspect was that they could be seriously stealthy when they wanted to be.

On another night he might have gone after her or maybe stayed up to think things through a bit more, but not this night. Tomorrow was a big day. He was exhausted and slipped back into a deep sleep.

CHAPTER SEVEN: *AL*

Al was tidying up the shop after a long day. Holiday weekends were always the busiest. Burgers, hot dogs, steaks, chicken wings, pork tenderloins, sausages, and a dozen other favorites went like hotcakes. Bob had finished mopping up the back a little while ago and had gone home.

Al would usually stay a bit longer to make sure everything up front was sparkling clean and ready to go for the next day. If you left the place a mess at night, it made it that much harder to get going in the morning.

Next to the closed cases of meats there was an open case of cheeses from around the world. Havarti from Denmark, Brie and d'Affinois from France, Stilton from England, and of course, a variety of American cheddars. It was amazing how many different flavors you could get from the milk of cows, goats, and sheep. They made for perfect appetizers and burger toppers for picnics.

Al wiped down the case and arranged the various orange, white, and blue blocks of cheese to maximize the overall composition and appeal of the display. There were cute little paper flags with the name and country of origin in each section to better help the customers decide on the perfect choice.

In the aisles of the store there were a variety of breads and dry pastas, pickled foods, and some crackers and cookies. Brightly colored boxes in every size imaginable sat beckoning.

Al was sweeping up in the dry goods area when the phone

rang. During the day you could hardly hear it, but now in the empty store it seemed very loud and broke the silence like a stone hitting a placid pond. He jumped a little and made his way back behind the counter again to answer it.

"Al and Bob's Meat Market, how can I help you?" It was after hours, but Al would always answer the phone in case someone wanted to place an order for pickup the next day.

"Oh, hi honey!" he said happily. It was Carol, his wife of thirty-two years. "Yes, just finishing up now. You're telling me! It was a busy day. We could barely keep the cases stocked."

Al continued to tidy up the knives and food prep area while he talked.

"Yes, the doctor did call back, but I didn't have much time to talk to him. Yes, he said the blood test results were back and that my cholesterol is very high. Well, yeah. Get this, he suggested cutting back on meat and dairy!" he said laughing. "I know, right? I told him he should come to our pig roast next week and maybe we can talk about some of those medications. Are the kids bringing the grandkids? Great."

The knives were neatly arranged now so he moved on to fluffing the prepared foods to even them out and make sure they are covered well.

"Yeah, he didn't know about the chest pains. He said it could be my heart, but it could also be heartburn or gas. I think it's just your mother's spicy casserole we've been putting down all week. That stuff could be used for mortar." He chuckled to himself as he recalled breaking a plastic serving spoon once trying to get it out of the dish.

"Yeah, I will. I'm almost done. I'll bring home that tri-tip steak for dinner tonight. Go ahead and fire up the grill." He made his way to the walk-in cooler in the back and picked up the large steak he had wrapped up earlier.

"Of course. I will. See you soon. I love you too."

Al hit the off button on the phone, ending the call with a beep. He paused for a moment to lean against the door of the meat cooler. Carol was the love of his life and made him smile every time he talked to her. He felt so blessed to be with her.

He was about to close the door to the cooler when that familiar chest pain came back. It felt like a little tightness at first - just a bit uncomfortable. Then he was a bit nauseous. He leaned his head on his arm and waited for it to pass. He would have to get some more antacids on the way home. He reached for the handle to close the door.

Then it became crushing and took his breath away.

His legs gave out and there was a loud smack as his head hit the floor. The phone hit the hard tile and broke apart. Small batteries exploded out of it and went rolling in different directions. He felt himself sweating and his entire body tightened up into a knot. He writhed in pain on the hard floor as he looked up at the bright fluorescent lights in the ceiling. The spring-loaded door kept trying to close on him as he pawed at the air in vain. It was hard to breathe, and the pain kept coming in waves.

He had never felt so helpless and scared. There was no one to help. He kept thinking of Carol. Her face. Her voice. She would be left all alone. He wished he could have more time with her. More time to live.

Everything started to go bright as he was losing consciousness. Is this really how it would end for him? He looked up and saw some of the sides of beef hanging from the ceiling just next to him. The red muscle and white bone. Parts of pigs suspended from metal hooks and chains. Carcasses and dead bodies. The pale round balls that were once chickens.

He had seen this all countless times before, but for some reason it was suddenly disturbing. He would soon become like them. Cold and lifeless. A piece of meat.

It was about this time that he was suddenly aware that he was not alone on the cold floor. Someone was feeling around at his neck. Maybe someone heard the noise and called 911? Was this a paramedic taking his pulse?

Shaking with pain and barely conscious, Al rolled his head to the side and saw something he did not expect at all. There was a furry-faced raccoon looking back at him. Any hopes he had at a rescue were dashed.

He laughed inwardly and barely managed to say "trash panda" quietly. It was just one of Bob's enemies come to raid the dumpster. The back door must have been ajar, and it worked its way in.

He felt a small pinch at his neck. Did it just bite him? Good Lord, he's not even dead yet and this thing was trying to eat him. He managed to pull his head and neck away with much effort.

Al then heard a voice say, "Stop struggling, I'm here to help you."

Now he was definitely sure this was the end. He was hallucinating and hearing voices. He turned his head back to the raccoon and saw it looking at him again. There was no mistake it was looking right at him. It had pulled its paws back and Al saw an odd-looking silver wristband on its left arm.

The white fog was still increasing, and he knew he was about to pass out. This was it. The end. There was a loud ringing in his ears and the shop seemed to be fading away. He thought he heard that voice again though. It sounded something like "make it count".

Then nothing.

CHAPTER EIGHT: *THE FIGHT*

*E*mma saw Ricky bolt out of the back of the market and run limping towards her.

"Did it work? Is he ok?" she asked as he approached quickly.

Ricky seemed to be avoiding looking up and almost ran right past Emma. She reached out and tried to slow him down.

"Hey, are you ok?" she asked with concern.

He snapped back to look at her. "NO, I am most certainly *not* ok! Let's get out of here."

Emma was very worried and confused, but the urgency in Ricky's voice made her hold back on asking anything more. They boarded the bike and she peddled hard as they traveled up and down the forested roads until they were home.

She rolled her bike up into the shed and Ricky sat down next to Monique, seemingly exhausted. His head was in his paws. Emma finally built up the courage to pry a bit more.

"Ricky, what's going on?" she asked.

Ricky looked up and she could see that he was mortified. "You didn't tell me he was a *butcher*."

"Of course he's a butcher – that's his shop," she replied.

"You mean he cuts up animals and serves them to other humans as food?" It wasn't really a question.

Emma seemed a little uncomfortable now, starting to understand why this might be a problem for Ricky. "Um, yes, I suppose that's accurate. But the animals come in already dead and he just prepares them. We don't eat raccoons or anything!

It's just the normal cows and chickens and pigs and things. We've been going there for years and he's really nice."

Ricky's mouth was agape. "And that makes it better?! If I brought in a box full of human parts and started cutting them up and putting them in little packages, you wouldn't find that upsetting?"

"Well, um…" Emma was struggling to find the right way to explain this.

"But they are already dead! So, it's ok!" Ricky had gotten up and was now wincing through the pain of his leg while circling around the inside of the shed. "He's only dealing in the suffering and death of countless animals for profit! Nothing wrong with that at all, especially if he's a nice guy."

"But raccoons eat meat too, just like humans you are omnivores," Emma said. This all seemed really strange to her and she was trying to work it all out.

Ricky's eyes were wide, and his paws outstretched. "Not anymore! Not when there is a choice! Being an omnivore means you *can* eat meat, not that you *have* to. No one has killed animals for food for hundreds of years in my time. How could you?" Ricky felt so conflicted he didn't know what to say.

When Monique said that Emma was different and kind to animals, he simply assumed she wouldn't be involved in such things. How can you be kind to some animals and then eat others?

Ricky briefly recalled the first glimpse he got of the market once he had picked the lock and gotten inside. It was cold, with hard wet tiles all around. He had looked around and saw *countless* dead bodies all around. They were everywhere. Bins full of body parts and blood.

It was like one of those silly horror movies the young kits would watch about how evil the long-lost humans were. But this was *real,* and it was appalling. At that moment, it was as if the floor had dropped out under Ricky's entire sense of purpose for the mission. This was the supremely important person that he was supposed to save? This *butcher*?

Emma sat motionless, feeling tears welling up in her eyes. She managed to speak softly, "But that's just how things are in *this* time. We have to eat too, and you can't expect…"

"What?" Ricky interjected shrilly while giving Emma a piercing look. "I can't expect humans to be compassionate or logical and eat something other than other animals? Why not? Do humans in your town *have* to eat animals to survive? Do you yourself *have* to?"

Emma glanced down at the floor as she answered. "No, we don't *have* to eat animals, but…"

"So it's a choice! It's because animals taste good, then?" Ricky said with incredulity. "Humans aren't even really omnivores in the same way that other animals are – you can't eat raw flesh without cooking it first. Your digestive tracts are almost identical to gorillas and other herbivores."

"But…" Emma tried to break in, but Ricky wasn't done.

"So, it's ok for this Al guy to cut up and serve once living and breathing and feeling animals because you like the taste of them?" he asked harshly. "And he's such a great guy because he smiles at you?"

Emma had had enough. She quickly got up and stormed out of the shed.

As she stepped down onto the stones in the yard, she slammed the door behind her without looking back. The sound of it was like a sudden crack of thunder that made Ricky jump. The door bounced back open with the force of the motion and gave Ricky a clear view of her walking away towards the brook.

Ricky looked at Monique and then off into the corner at nothing in particular.

Monique finally broke the silence. "She's right you know. You can't expect people of this time to fit into the ideals and mindset of your time. They just aren't there yet. *We* aren't there yet," she said softly and in a way that was soothing.

Ricky looked through the open doorway towards the brook and saw Emma sitting on a fallen tree. Her head was in her hands and moving haltingly up and down. She was sobbing.

Ricky felt his heart become heavy in his chest.

"Oh, crumbs," he said regretfully.

Monique continued, "She doesn't deserve to be made to feel that way. She's just a kid, and the nicest human I've ever met. She saved your life in fact. Give her time."

Ricky knew she was right, but still felt conflicted about the entire situation. It was like being ordered to save the life of a mass murderer. And then you find out your friend is an accomplice to many of those murders.

He knew what he had to do, but it didn't make it any easier. Monique smiled at him in her knowing way and surprised him by putting her arms around him in a warm embrace. Closing his eyes, he gave up the last of his resistance and melted in her soft fur.

"Thank you," he said as he finally pulled away. Monique nodded with a smile and pulled her hands back to her chest as if hugging herself too. He nudged a bit of wet fur under his eyes with his black paws and smiled back at her.

Ricky took a deep breath and hobbled his way towards Emma's spot on the brook. It was slow going with his entire leg wrapped up the way it was, but he was determined to make it. His striped tail swished back and forth as he went.

Emma looked up with a start as he got closer. Her eyes were red, and her pretty face went quickly from a look of utter sadness to a scowl of anger.

"I don't want to talk to you," she barked.

"That's understandable," Ricky said softly as he climbed up on the log and sat down next to her. She didn't move away, which gave him a bit of hope.

"I shouldn't have gotten so mad. I'm sorry," he said sincerely.

Emma took a moment to look in Ricky's direction and nodded a little.

"I was just so unprepared for what I saw in there," Ricky said. "So much death. It was everywhere. I think what made it worse was how normal it seemed. The shop was so cheerful in one area with bright signs and happy little displays of boxes and treats. But just on the other side and in the cold room was such utter horror."

Ricky looked around as if seeing the scene again in his mind. "Every one of those animals was once a warm, breathing, living creature with thoughts and feelings of its own. But in that place, they were reduced to the value of the weight of their muscle tissue. For the simple taste of it."

Emma listened intently as Ricky continued.

"Eating all of that meat is not even good for humans – it's not healthy. My wristband reported the scanned data from Al, and it showed that decades of eating animals was the cause of his "natural" death. He had extra weight and clogged arteries that were making his heart work way too hard. He also had the beginning stages of colon cancer."

"What did you do to save him, anyway?" Emma asked.

"I injected him with some nano drones. They are tiny machines that can carry out whatever program you send to them."

"What do they do?"

"In this case, it was a standard life-saving protocol to remove the arterial plaque, enhance the heart muscle, repair any damaged tissues, stop cancer growth, and correct any imbalances in his entire system," Ricky said.

"That won't hurt him?" Emma asked.

Ricky laughed. "Not at all. He probably feels better now than he ever has. Even in my time that kind of treatment is exceedingly rare and valuable. If I had any more to spare, I would have used them for my own injuries."

Emma was still reeling from the situation. "He really is a nice guy. He's not evil or anything. That's just the way things are in this time," she said.

Ricky tried to think of a way to explain his perspective. "Do you remember how you felt when you thought I was about to kill Al with the nano pen injection?"

Emma nodded.

"Well," he said, "that's how you felt when someone you cared about was threatened. It didn't matter that it was me, someone nice, someone you know, doing the threatening."

Emma was trying to stick with this metaphor as he continued.

"So, imagine you have a group of a hundred friends, and you see their bodies after they are murdered. It doesn't matter that the person who did it is outwardly friendly. It's still a traumatic experience," he said.

"I guess," she replied.

Ricky continued. "In my time, every living animal is treated as an equal. We all do our best to get along and to love one another. It doesn't matter if we look different or have different opinions about things – we are all one family."

Emma was still skeptical. "Every living creature? Even insects?" she asked as she eyed a mosquito hovering just outside of the window.

"Well… we all do our best with the insects, but they are certainly a challenge at times. They have ambassadors that we are working with to improve relations, but the best policy with them has been to leave them alone as much as possible. We are very different after all," he said.

Ricky scratched at his right arm distractedly as if remembering something from his past. "I'm no fan of ticks, myself. But mammals are so similar. *We* are so similar. In my time it is unthinkable that any of us would harm another intentionally. So, seeing this level of abuse on an industrial scale is just unfathomable."

He gazed up at her face and admired her green eyes as she looked back. "I've seen how caring you are. I know how thoughtful you are. You spoke so highly of this Al person. I just don't get it."

"Get what?" Emma asked.

"How can you kill and eat animals when you don't have to? Especially when it is so bad for the animals, for you, and for your planet on the whole? Every pound of animal flesh takes a huge amount of land, water, feed, and energy to produce."

Ricky exhaled sharply and looked as if he were pondering something serious.

"I'm not supposed to tell you this, but later this year, the Amazon rainforest in Brazil will be decimated by fires. But not the natural kind – these will be *deliberately* set by farmers and ranchers just so that they can move cattle in to be raised and slaughtered. How is that ok? How is *any* of this ok?"

Emma had to think about it for a moment. Why *was* it ok to kill and eat animals? Or to use them for any purpose? She thought about Herbert the frog from her science class. Did he really have to die? What was the benefit? They were handing those frogs out as if they had no value other than what they could do for humans.

And, sure, some animals taste really good, but at what cost? Not only does the animal have to suffer and die, but the health of whoever eats it can be affected negatively. The impact on the planet is obviously catastrophic as well.

She thought about her own history and finally came up with a few thoughts from her own life.

"That's just how it is right now," she said. "I don't even do the food shopping, my dad does. Before Mom died, she did. I eat what they prepare. The same thing happens at school – I don't get a choice to not eat meat. It's just what they give me. That's what's normal."

Ricky understood a bit, but still had questions about how this could possibly be acceptable. "Do you know where meat comes from? Do you ever see what happens to the animals before they are cut up and delivered?"

"No, not really," she said honestly. "If you travel you sometimes see cows on farms. Everyone knows in some abstract way that meat comes from animals, but honestly most of us don't think about it that much. Not the details of it anyway."

"That's *cognitive dissonance*," Ricky said. "Whenever you are presented with information that goes contrary to how you see yourself, instead of changing your views or actions, you simply don't think about it. It's easier that way."

Emma thought about that for a moment. "Yeah, that sounds about right. But why think about terrible things you can't change?"

Ricky smiled. "That's what my mission is all about – you *can* change. All of you. Almost every human here in this country is making a choice to eat or not to eat meat. How many people would still eat meat if they had to kill and dismember the living animal themselves?"

Emma scrunched her mouth to the side in a funny but thoughtful look. "Hmmm… I know some hunters do that, but the vast majority of people can't even bring themselves to think about that or see photos of what actually happens. We just see the packages in the store."

Emma then recalled something she saw in the store recently. "Some of those packages say 'humanely raised' or something similar. Doesn't that help?" she asked hopefully.

"Not really," Ricky said. "Going back in your own human history, that's like saying that some slaves had nice rooms, so it's all ok. It's really not, no matter how you phrase it. They are unwilling victims."

"Ok, but aren't they important to the planet too?" Emma asked. "I saw a movie once where these nice people created their own farm and they needed animals to bring the soil back so that they could grow crops naturally. The animals were a part of the balance."

"Yes," Ricky said, nodding his head, "animals are indeed a part of the natural order of life on the planet and are vital to ecosystems. But the lives of the vast majority of these animals that are killed for meat are nowhere near as nice as you might think."

"There aren't any happy animals on little farms somewhere? Or maybe we could eat them after they die a natural death?" Emma asked hopefully.

"That's within the realm of possibility, but a happy cow, pig, or chicken on a small farm is *not* the reality for most of meat production. And usually when an animal dies a natural death, they are considered contaminated. Therefore, slaughtering healthy, young animals is the norm."

Ricky looked at the water in the brook for a moment and exhaled deeply. "Here, let me show you something."

Ricky held out his wristband and quickly punched a few different commands into it. A glowing rectangle of light began to emanate a few inches above his wrist. It looked like that hologram of Princess Leia in *Star Wars*, but a bit bigger and much more high-resolution.

"Wow, that's really cool!" Emma exclaimed. Ricky thought it was nice to see her sense of wonder and amazement at something that was so commonplace for him.

"Get ready," Ricky said. "This is a short interactive video about where your meat comes from."

Emma suddenly wasn't so sure she wanted to see it, but she also wanted to show that she could handle the facts. If this was the reality of things, she needed to know.

On the 3D projection, Emma saw a short video playing out. It took her a few seconds to figure out what was going on. At first, it showed a family eating dinner around a small table. The meal was some kind of meatloaf that three kids and a man were eating. Then it started playing in reverse, as if someone was holding the rewind button down. It was a little disorienting, but Emma was getting the gist of it and processed the scenes in her mind.

The video spooled back to the mother in the kitchen opening a package of ground beef and mixing it together in a bowl with some eggs and other ingredients. The scene faded to black and some plain white text appeared asking a question:

Would you do this? YES / NO

"I don't understand," Emma said with a furrowed brow.
Ricky gestured to the text with his other paw. "Use your

finger and select your answer. It's asking if you are ok with what you are seeing in this particular scene."

"If I'm ok with it?" she asked, hoping for a bit more clarification.

"Yes, the program is asking if you are ok with it, in a moral sense," Ricky replied. "Like, is the mother harming the family or doing something bad. Or put another way, would you do what the human is doing in the scene at that moment?"

"Oh, ok," Emma said. "Well, I know we are talking about the problems of meat and such, and I think the husband should probably do his part to make dinner too, but I wouldn't say that the mother is doing anything terrible here." Emma looked towards Ricky to see if he agreed, but his face was neutral. If he was showing any expression it was deep beneath his mask of black and reddish-brown fur.

Emma continued explaining her train of thought. "She has cooked a meal for her family that obviously needs to eat. I'd do this, so I'll go with the *yes* answer." She poked the large YES text with her finger and there was a soft beep sound that confirmed the program had accepted her choice.

"Is that it?" Emma asked.

Ricky shook his head and the video continued. In the next scene, it showed the mother from the kitchen scene, but this time it was earlier in the day and she was picking that same package of meat out of a refrigerated case in a large food store. She had put it into her cart with her other groceries. The scene again faded to black and the question reappeared.

Would you do this? YES / NO

"Um, sure," Emma said. "That's pretty normal human behavior right there." Again, she poked the *yes* option and the soft beep sounded. Emma was starting to understand that this was going to proceed in a likewise fashion for a bit.

The next few scenes were a quick blur of workers placing the meat package into the case, and then the video spooled backwards again to show them taking it out of a larger cardboard box. The video spooled back again, and Emma could see the workers unloading the larger box from a refrigerated truck. Then it played in reverse again to show the truck's travels across the country. The truck portion was a sped-up bit that showed the package moving across many highways.

Would you do this? YES / NO

"Well, the truck is causing some pollution of course, and it's not exactly my dream job, but I could do that. It's just the delivery and the store workers putting items out," Emma said. She punched the *yes* choice and it proceeded.

The next scene was at an enormous metal clad building in some open farmland. Inside, the actual meat package made its way from the large cardboard box on a conveyor belt, backwards towards a large silver machine. It was a grinder of some kind. At the top, a worker was tossing large chunks of red meat in, while at the bottom, a mushy paste of ground meat pressed out and into neat little packages.

Another worker took each styrofoam package that was wrapped in plastic and stamped it with a white label, sending the package on its way towards the boxing area. Going back to the worker at the top, the video showed a conveyor belt that fed them the chunks that were tossed into the grinder.

Would you do this? YES / NO

"Ah, well this is more of the behind the scenes kind of stuff, like they do in the back at the butcher's shop," Emma said. "Whether someone is doing it by hand in a local store or in a larger setting though it's pretty much the same thing. I wouldn't be thrilled about it, but I guess I'd have to go with *yes*." Her hand moved a little slower towards the yes button this time, but the now familiar beep sounded and the video proceeded.

In the next scene, it showed the area at the very beginning of the conveyor belt where there were some very large white bins that held all of the chunks of meat. They came from another enormous room that the video now proceeded to show. In this room, there were rows after rows of hanging carcasses of cows. Workers were taking them off of large hooks on a chain-fed line to cut them apart on large tables. There were bins for various parts and streams of blood ran into drains in the tables and floor.

Emma was starting to feel a little sickened by all of this and looked up at Ricky. He looked apologetic but nodded towards the video for her to finish.

Would you do this? YES / NO

"Um, yeah, this is getting a little graphic here," Emma said with disgust starting to creep into her expression. "This is the kind of stuff that most people just turn away from," she said. "We might get glimpses of it, but we try not to think about it too much."

"So, is this something that most humans are ok with?" Ricky asked. "If you were there, would you do this yourself?"

Emma paused to think about it for a bit. "I don't think most people would want to be there, but at the same time they probably wouldn't stop the workers either. That being said, if I had to do that myself, I would quit. I would never want to do that. I'm choosing *no*." This time, she punched the *no* choice and a slightly different beep sounded. She had hoped that maybe choosing the *no* option would stop the video, but it proceeded unabated.

The video played on to show what happened before the last scene. Emma saw how two sides of beef were originally together before being cut apart with a band saw, and before that the head, feet, and skin were removed. It was hard to take in, so she watched through half-closed eyes.

Would you do this? YES / NO

"Ok, I get your point," Emma said, feeling a bit of sweat on her palms as she rubbed them on the rough bark of the tree below her. "This is something I would never want to do. I had a hard enough time slicing into a frog in my bio class. I would never voluntarily cut an animal like a cow in half with a saw, or cut off its limbs, even if it is already dead. Definitely *no*." She pressed her choice and looked somewhat uncomfortable when the video continued.

In another area that must have been the actual slaughterhouse, she saw in reverse the actual living cow being channeled through various gates. There was a section of the room that had a worker holding a gun-like device that was firing a metal bolt of some kind through the heads of each cow that was led through. That must have been what actually killed them. Emma flinched each time it fired.

In another section there was a man with a large knife that was manually slitting the necks of some cows. The cows were very much alive and choked on the blood as they tried to break free. She had heard that this was how some meat was deemed religiously "better", but it hardly seemed kinder in any way.

Would you do this? YES / NO

"Nope!" Emma said firmly as she held both hands up in front of her. "I don't care how much you pay me; I'm not going to fire a bolt gun at a cow's head or slice a cow's throat. If I saw someone doing this in front of me, I'd want to stop them." She punched the *no* choice quickly, but the video continued.

Finally, the video left the slaughterhouse and she saw the cows being led through various chutes and gates from an enormous barn. Emma breathed a small sigh of relief – the worst was over.

Only it wasn't. The video continued and inside the barn she saw countless cows, technically steers and heifers, packed into small pens so tightly they could barely move. Newborn calves were being removed immediately from their crying mothers by workers. Feed mixed with antibiotics and vitamins was distributed through long troughs. Excrement and mud were splattered almost everywhere. Workers with long plastic gloves were artificially inseminating cows in one area. Other cows that had recently given birth were attached to pumps to remove the milk that the calves never got.

The workers were very rough with the animals as well – poking them, pulling at them, prodding at them with electric poles. It was obvious that the cows lived their entire lives in this building.

The video stopped to show one particular cow in a narrow pen. It had no name, but there was a numbered tag that was attached through its ear with a metal clip. Flies buzzed around its head but it didn't move.

Emma looked up at Ricky as the video lingered on the single cow. "Why did the video stop to show this one?" she asked softly.

"She is the cow that becomes the meatloaf," Ricky said sorrowfully.

Emma looked back at the screen. The lone cow looked scared and broken.

It was overwhelmingly sad.

Would you do this? YES / NO

Emma slowly touched the *no* choice as a tear rolled down her cheek.

The video now jumped back to that family from the beginning of the film. The children didn't seem to be very happy with the meatloaf, so the mother took a large portion of it and dumped it in the trashcan. The video went blank and the light from the wristband disappeared.

Emma was speechless.

Ricky saw her expression and felt sorry for showing it to her, but knew it had to be done.

"That's not even the entire video," he said quietly. "It goes on to show where the eggs came from. In factory farms they grind the beaks off of the chickens so that they won't fight, and since male chicks are considered useless, they are tossed into a huge grinder…"

"Oh, dear God, no," Emma said tearfully. "Please stop."

"Ok," Ricky said as he covered the wristband with his paw as if to hide it away.

"I'm sorry. But do you see why I was so upset about the butcher shop?" Ricky asked. "Every time you see meat somewhere in a nice little display case, chances are it came from a place like this."

"Is it all like this?" Emma asked.

"The vast majority. Roughly ninety-nine percent of meat, dairy, and eggs in this country come from factory farms. Even if the marketing sticker says that it was humanely raised, these animals don't have a choice."

Ricky paused to look at a small bird that was flitting from branch to branch cheerfully on the other side of the brook. It must not have seen the video.

"Maybe they get to go outside sometimes," he said. "Or maybe they are exceedingly lucky to have a better life on a smaller farm with humans who treat them well, but the simple truth is that they never volunteered for this and they have no say."

"I guess you're right," Emma said. "It's not right for us to treat other living beings like this when there are other options."

Ricky looked back at the bird as one of its friends flew over to join it. "If humans, or even dogs or cats were treated like this, people would be up in arms in the streets, right?"

"That's for sure," she said. "I guess it's a pretty weird when you think about it."

"Yes," Ricky said. "It's not right for any living, feeling creature to be treated like this. And the average person in this country is responsible for the slaughter of roughly one hundred animals per year."

"I never knew it was really that bad," Emma said. "As I mentioned before, it seems that we try not to think about it," she said as she wiped away the tears from her face.

"But that doesn't mean it isn't happening," Ricky said. "You wouldn't do those things yourself, but by buying meat you are paying someone else to do all of those things for you."

Emma was nodding her head. "I understand now."

"Every time you buy some meat you are supporting this," Ricky said. "I don't know how it ever got to be so acceptable. How did this become the norm?" Ricky asked, really wanting to understand.

Emma thought about it for a moment. "At one point in our history that might have been the only way to survive."

"But is that still the case for you today?" Ricky asked.

"No," Emma said honestly. She thought about Al's shop and her own family again.

"I think it's just how we are raised," she said. "Al has a bunch of photos in his shop of his father and grandfather, who also were butchers. We pass it on to our children as normal, and so that's what they do."

"And what about in your own family and life?"

"It's just like Mom and Dad cooking meals for me and school lunches – that's just what was normal. If your parents ate meat and fed you meat your entire life you would probably continue to eat it too."

"Maybe," Ricky said. He didn't want to think that he would do such a thing, but society can have many pressures.

Ricky put his soft paw on Emma's hand. "At some point, for the sake of the planet and all of the life that depends on it, everyone must make their *own* decisions and choose the right path," he said seriously.

Emma nodded and Ricky pulled his paw back, using it to

once again cover the wristband. They both looked at the brook and listened to the calming sound of the water and the birds all around them for a few moments.

A gentle breeze made Emma's hair dance around the frame of her face and she turned towards the sun to take in its warmth. She rocked a little on the log and looked back towards Ricky.

"Have you ever eaten meat?" Emma asked. "I hate to say it, but it does taste really good. I suppose that makes it even more difficult for people to give it up," she said, hoping not to offend Ricky.

Ricky smiled. "Of course I've had meat before, and I do like the taste of it, but not *killed* meat. We have what you might call *cultured meat* or *clean meat*."

"How is that different?" Emma asked.

"Cells from a willing donor are harvested painlessly and cultured to form tissue. That tissue is then cooked and served. It doesn't kill the original donor, it's way better for the environment, and can be engineered to be even more healthy and tasty," Ricky said.

"Is that how carnivores eat in your time?" Emma asked.

"Yes, that's exactly right," Ricky said. "Some animals, like cats, are obligate carnivores, so they don't have a choice – they have to eat meat."

"Yeah, I've never heard of a vegan cat," Emma said lightheartedly.

"True! But there's absolutely no reason why it has to be killed meat. It's the same nutrients, just without the suffering and much less of an environmental impact."

Emma thought about the possibilities for a moment. "Is it the same animals in the future that donate cells, like cows and chickens and pigs?"

"Yes, among many others. There are actually a few amazing hybrid meats that my mom used to cook, and you can even eat raccoon meat if you really want to."

"Ugh, gross!" Emma exclaimed, making a repulsed face.

Ricky looked surprised. "In what way is it more gross to eat tissue from a willing raccoon donor than to kill and dismember an unwilling victim like a cow?"

"I guess you're right," she said. "But that relates to your societal norm. For you maybe it's totally normal, but for me it's super gross." She scrunched her face with an expression of mixed disgust and curiosity. "What does raccoon even taste like?"

"I haven't actually tried it," Ricky said. "Most of us prefer fresh grains and fruits and vegetables. I have a few clean meat favorites too. But there are always a few eccentrics who want something unusual, and as long as no one gets hurt I don't object."

"I can't imagine eating raccoon meat," Emma said with a slight smirk.

"Well, if you really want to try some, I suppose you can eat me if I die on this mission," Ricky said with a little laugh. "I give you permission."

"Absolutely not! That is not even remotely funny," Emma said as she found herself laughing involuntarily.

"Yeah, you're right. I might be a little gamey," Ricky replied with a chuckle.

They both laughed a bit and took a moment to again look at the water falling over the rocks in the brook.

After a few moments, Emma's face got more serious. "I sure don't want you do die on this mission. I want humans and animals to get along better. And I want to help you to do it."

Ricky looked at her with admiration. Even after he yelled at her and showed her some of the most horrific footage he had ever seen, she still wanted to help. She could have turned away and told him to do this on his own, but she didn't. Maybe Monique was right after all. Maybe this girl is different.

"Thank you, Emma," he said.

"You're welcome," she said with a slowly brightening smile. It was good to see her smiling again.

Ricky breathed a sigh of relief and tossed a small rock into the brook. It broke the water of a small pool with a splash. "Fortunately, we have a few days until the next target is due, so I will be able to do some more reconnaissance on this one and hopefully not encounter any more surprises."

"That's good, since my dad's picnic is tomorrow, and I may be tied up with that," she said.

The thought of meat suddenly came back to Ricky. "Maybe… you can find some alternative food options?" he asked with hope.

Emma caught on quickly this time. "Yes, I'll see if I can get dad to buy some veggie burgers or something."

"That would be great. And maybe… some more of those black and white cookies too?" he asked with a smile and raised eyebrows.

"You got it," she replied with an even broader smile. She leaned over and put her arm around Ricky.

He leaned back into her and started to feel much better about everything.

CHAPTER NINE: *CHANGES*

Al woke up feeling very disoriented and confused. The cold air from the meat cooler was spilling over him as he lay on the hard tile floor. Like waking from a nightmare, he was having a difficult time remembering what had happened. Something bad. Something terrible. He instinctively grabbed for his chest and started to remember the details.

The blinding pain - a heart attack. Hitting his head on the floor. He thought he was going to die. He remembered seeing the hanging bodies of meat and thinking of Carol.

He wiped the sweat off of his brow and collected his thoughts. As he started to regain his composure, he looked around on the floor for the batteries for the phone. He popped them into place and was startled when it started ringing almost instantly.

"Uh, hello?" he said weakly. It was Carol. He put his head in his other hand and almost wept at hearing her voice.

"Yes, I'm fine." He wasn't sure what he should say and scrambled to find something suitable. "I just got held up with an order. No, I'm not sure why the phone didn't ring when you called. But everything's ok. I'm headed home right now. I love you too."

Looking up, Al hung up the phone and sat on the cold floor. He wasn't exactly sure what to make of all of this. He knew he had almost died – it was unmistakable. What he felt was no heartburn or indigestion. It was like he had been hit by a truck.

But now he felt fine. He took a moment and realized that he didn't just feel fine, but *great*. Like he was twenty years younger. His chest and head didn't hurt at all. His vision was sharp and crisp. He inhaled deeply and picked out a half dozen distinct smells. He heard the fans of the refrigeration units running. One of them was slightly off-balance and was thrumming a frequency vibration that waxed and waned. His mind cleared and he felt calm and focused.

He recalled more of the events that led up to the attack – cleaning the store, talking to Carol, and picking up the meat for dinner. Then there was that voice that said, *'make it count'*.

The trash panda, the raccoon was there. It was almost as if it had saved him. He looked around but didn't see it anymore. He was alone with the cold bodies of the other animals in the cooler. He didn't want to look at them.

Should he go to the hospital? He didn't feel like he needed it. He would call the doctor tomorrow. Apart from feeling much better, something else was different about Al. He knew he needed to make some changes in his own life. He also made a mental note to talk to Bob about some changes for the market.

That, and to discuss those trash pandas that like to come around at night.

CHAPTER TEN: *THE BACKUP*

Ricky awoke to the now familiar squeeze of the proximity alarm from his wristband again. He looked around and saw only blackness. His keen ears listened intently, but he only heard the chirping of crickets and frogs outside in the warm night.

This time he had a feeling he knew what was coming, so he punched a small button on the side of his wristband. A bright white light suddenly beamed out of his wristband and illuminated half of the shed's interior.

"Ack!" Minka cried as she cringed away from the light.

"I figured you would be coming back to gloat," Ricky said.

Minka's silky black fur was reflecting the light and she squinted as she brought her white paw up to shield her narrowing cat eyes. Ricky lowered the light a little. He looked over and saw that Monique was sound asleep again – did anything wake her up?

"Hey trash panda. Did you like what you saw at the butcher's shop?" she asked wryly.

"Not particularly," Ricky said. It was definitely an understatement, but there was no sense in giving her the satisfaction of a big response. "And what's with the 'trash panda' bit? The butcher said that too."

"It's just a nickname for raccoons. I like it actually. Kinda like my rabbit friend I call a 'boople snoot' and my skunk friend that I call a 'fart squirrel.'"

Ricky had to stifle a laugh at hearing that one.

"It's best just to own a nickname like that and embrace it," Minka said. "Speaking of squirrels, farting or otherwise, I thought you should know that I have a friend who said you would be coming." She slunk in a relaxed way to sit next to Ricky's bed. She licked her paw and ran it over her ears as if nothing were bothering her at all now.

Ricky tried hard to hide his confusion but wasn't sure it was working. "What do you mean?" he asked.

"A little squirrel told me that you would be coming here. To this *time*," she said with emphasis as she eyed him carefully.

Ricky's face showed a sudden expression of shock. "Wait a second, that could only mean that…"

"Yes, I see you putting it together now. I know you aren't the first time traveler to come here to this time on this particular mission. You are, in fact, the *third*," she said pointedly.

It stung significantly to be reminded that he wasn't the first choice for this mission. That's why his training was so rushed – he was the backup. The emergency reserve.

"I know that the first two travelers failed and were never heard from again. We don't even know if they made the jump successfully," Ricky said.

"Well, they made it here, and one of them would love to talk to you. I'll send him by tomorrow. His name is Jake, but I suppose you already know that," she said.

Ricky did indeed. Jake and Isabelle were the two squirrel agents sent as a team. They were a cute couple actually – very dedicated. He had known them for quite some time while the two of them were training together. When it came time for Ricky's own training, Ricky only had a few days by himself.

"What did Jake say about the mission?" Ricky asked while looking over at Monique to see if she was still asleep. She was.

But there was no response. Just like that, Minka had vanished again.

"Bye then," Ricky said sarcastically as he passed the light around the shed to confirm she was indeed gone. Is this what passed for manners in this time?

Ricky clicked off the light and was left to the silence, the darkness, and his thoughts about the mission. Did this change anything? Why didn't Jake and Isabelle complete the mission? Had there been a malfunction of some kind?

On the topic of the mission, Ricky was still very troubled. Why was he sent to save Al the butcher? Now that he had saved him, won't he just go on to contribute more to the very problem the mission was designed to stop? Even if Al closed up his shop, it's not like he is a major distributor or something. Why go through the trouble?

Ricky pulled his blanket up and tried to sleep, but for the rest of the night he kept waking up. His mind kept turning things over and over. He knew that trusting in the mission was the best way to go, but something just felt wrong.

He kept telling himself he didn't have much of a choice. No choice really. Or did he?

Ricky's own words kept playing back in his mind. *"At some point, for the sake of the planet and all of the life that depends on it, everyone must make their own decisions and choose the right path."*

"Oh crumbs," he said softly. "This is getting complicated."

PART THREE: THE HUNTER

CHAPTER ELEVEN: *JAKE*

It was the day of the big picnic for Emma and her dad. The sun was shining, white fluffy clouds floated past lazily, and Ricky watched from a distance as Emma's dad fought with the grill.

He kept rotating a large black knob that made a clicking sound. He turned it one way until the clicking started, and then after a few moments turned it back the other way. Again to the clicking sound. Again back the other way.

After a few times of repeating this, there was a loud "poof" sound and a flash of orange flame that encompassed the entire grill. Emma's dad reeled backwards and exclaimed some words that Ricky had never heard before. He rubbed his eyebrows with both hands and then inspected the underside of the grill. After a bit he walked grumpily back into the house.

A few minutes later, Emma came out and sat down with Ricky in between some pine trees. The sound of water flowing over the brook made for a peaceful backdrop to their conversation.

"It looks like some critters chewed through the gas lines on the grill, so I'll be heading to the hardware store with my dad. We will also get some non-meat burgers," she said as she picked up a small white stone that looked like quartz. She turned it over in her hands and felt the smooth edges.

"Ok," Ricky replied.

"We are leaving soon once my dad recovers a little," Emma said with a smirk. "Now that Al has been saved, who is your next target?"

It seemed like a good time to review things. Ricky raised up his wristband and tapped it a few times with his dexterous raccoon paw. The display showed the next part of the mission in bright blue letters:

R. WOODMAN
41.383N, -73.025W
5.28.2019
07:42 HRS
METHOD: INTERVENE

Emma looked at the information. "That's tomorrow. Today is a holiday, Memorial Day, that's why I'm not in school, but tomorrow I have to go back. I recognize the name though – my classmate Billy's last name is Woodman. He lives with his mom, but his dad lives nearby," Emma said.

She placed the white stone down and pulled out her phone. She then punched in the coordinates and saw that they indicated a spot somewhat in the middle of the woods. "What does it mean, 'Intervene'?"

"It means that I need to be there at that time and do whatever I can to save the target. No nano pen injection this time, just render whatever aid I can," Ricky said.

"Don't you have any more details on what will happen?" Emma asked.

"Unfortunately, no. Too many details will jeopardize the mission, so things are kept as simple as possible. I will have to assess what I see and try to save the target however I can," Ricky replied.

"Will you be able to make it ok on your own? Maybe I could fake being sick or something…" Emma said with a bit of optimism at the thought of skipping school for a good reason.

"No, school is important, and you should go. I'll leave early so that there will be plenty of time for me to get there," Ricky said. His injury worried him a little, but he was hoping that he could still handle whatever action the situation called for.

"Ok, well I have to go now, but I'll be back soon," Emma said cheerfully. "I'll see you in a bit?"

"Looking forward to it." Ricky said with a smile. She reached out and gave the soft fur around his ears a pat.

Ricky watched her walk back to the house and bounce up the steps inside. He was surprised how much he liked Emma and felt somewhat sad that she had to leave.

He was headed back towards the shed to see if Monique was there, when he heard someone approaching through the garden. His proximity alarm gave a squeeze on his wrist.

"Hey old friend," he heard from a familiar voice coming from the hosta plants. He knew right away it was Jake the squirrel – the initial time traveler agent sent on this mission.

He looked over, and sure enough – there was Jake. Grey and brown fur, white belly, fluffy tail. He wasn't sure what to say, but it was good to see him again.

"Jake! I can't believe it's really you," Ricky said.

"It's me all right," Jake said with a smirk while hopping closer. They met and embraced. It was good to be back in touch with someone from the same time - there was some deep connection because of that. Ricky had to focus on the mission though.

"What happened? Are you and Isabelle ok?" he asked.

Jake's chipper face suddenly turned serious. He looked at Ricky from the side as if he couldn't meet his gaze. "Isabelle is gone. The mission is a farce," he said grimly.

Ricky wasn't sure what to make of that. "What do you mean?"

"I saw you save the butcher. You shouldn't have done that," Jake said.

"I don't understand," Ricky said. "That is the mission."

Jake sat back on his hind legs. "I know that was the mission, but the mission is flawed. There was a mistake," he said as he looked off into the distance.

Ricky had a dozen questions he wanted to ask, but it seemed prudent to let Jake continue at his own pace.

After a moment, Jake did continue. "That man is a butcher. A murderer of animals. We are not supposed to *save* men like that, we are supposed to *stop* them."

Hearing this from Jake triggered some of Ricky's own questions. Was the mission really flawed?

"Have you scoped out the other two targets yet?" Jake asked.

"Not yet," Ricky replied. "I suffered an injury during transport, and it has slowed me down a little." He gestured to his leg and Jake acknowledged it with a nod.

"The next two are even worse," Jake said seriously.

Ricky wasn't sure how the next targets could be worse than the butcher and what he had seen in the shop, but he was suddenly afraid of what might be to come.

"Come with me and I'll show you," Jake said as he pulsed his tail and hopped towards the brook.

Ricky wanted to take some time to think things through, but since scoping out the next target was his highest priority, it seemed appropriate to go along with Jake.

He looked around for Monique, but she was nowhere to be seen.

"Ok, lead the way," Ricky said, trying to be braver than he felt.

Slowly they made their way through the woods, mostly following the small brook upstream. It probably wasn't that far, but with Ricky's injured leg it seemed like miles and miles.

Eventually they came to a large pine grove where the maples and underbrush gave way to fragrant needles and short ground cover. The sun was still shining far above with crows calling in the distance, but here down below it was shaded and quiet.

Just over a small hill there was a wooden cabin that came into view. It had rough timber walls, a small porch that wrapped around the front and the side, and a metal roof with long seams. A silver smokestack poked out of the main roof, and there was also a satellite dish of some kind. A small building in the back had an additional brick chimney, through which grey and black smoke poured in a steady stream. It smelled of burning wood and something else that Ricky couldn't quite identify.

"This is the place," Jake said as he pointed down the small hill to the cabin. "Randall Woodman is the target. He should be home soon."

Ricky spent a few moments taking in the scene. On the front porch was a bench suspended from the roof, and below it was a large brown dog with a chain attached to its collar. The bench moved slightly in the breeze while the dog slept below it. Nearby there was a wooden doghouse with "Rosco" painted crudely above the door. Piles of firewood lay around, and there was a splitting maul stuck into a tree stump next to one of them.

After a little while, they heard an approaching sound that got louder and more distinctive as it got closer. The dog's ears perked up too. Eventually a flat gray pickup truck came into view, bouncing towards them on the dirt road that led to the cabin. Over the sound of the truck's engine and burbling exhaust, there was the tinny sound of loud music coming from within the vehicle.

The large truck zoomed by quickly and skidded to a halt on the gravel just before the cabin's porch. It had tires that looked bigger than any that Ricky had ever seen, and the sides of the truck were splattered with dried mud.

The dog was pulling at the chain by this point, excitedly barking and jumping around. Randall Woodman shut off the engine of the truck, and then silenced the twangy radio music with a click. Ricky noticed that in the back of the truck there were a variety of tools and trash.

There were also some flag stickers on the bumper. One he recognized as the symbol of the United States of America from this time, as well as another with different stars and stripes in more of an "X" pattern. Another sticker on the back window said, "Keep Calm and Carry On!" in large letters. It was accompanied by an image of a handgun. Ricky vaguely recognized the saying as something important to humans but had no idea what it meant in this context.

Randall got out of the truck and closed the door with a squeaky bang. "Hey Rosco! Did you miss me?" he said playfully as he got closer to the dog and porch. Rosco the dog was just about losing his mind by this point and was nearly choking himself on the chain to reach the human.

"Ok, ok, here ya go," Randall said as he unhooked Rosco's chain. The dog nearly bowled him over and kept up an impressive barrage of barking and licking. The human hugged him back. "I missed you too, buddy. Go hunt up some squirrels or a coon while I relax and get dinner ready. Go!" With this he pointed off into the woods and the dog obediently disappeared in a blur of motion.

Randall picked up a dirty set of work clothes from the back of the truck and also a helmet that had reflective yellow tape on it. Ricky saw that there was a yellowish jacket with "R. Woodman" on the back in reflective orange letters. He also picked up a set of very large black boots and thick gloves.

"He's a fireman," Jake said.

"What does that mean?" Ricky asked as he continued to look at the objects in the truck bed.

"When something catches on fire," Jake replied, "he's one of the humans that comes and puts it out."

Ricky nodded with understanding. There were of course animals that served this purpose in their time, but naturally they weren't called "firemen" and they didn't need such primitive gear.

Randall stepped up the creaky wooden steps into the cabin while carrying his clothes, and a few moments later Ricky and Jake heard the sound of talking and music coming from inside. They made their way a little closer to get a better look.

Ricky couldn't see much in the way of details, but he was able to make out that Randall had opened up the large white refrigerator and pulled out a bundle of silver cans. He proceeded to open one of them with his fingers, which resulted in a hissing sound, followed by a louder crack and a small spray of foam. He slumped down in a large chair while quickly draining the first can.

"He watches TV for hours on end after work. In fact, that's his greatest weakness," Jake said.

"What do you mean, weakness?" Ricky asked, somewhat perplexed.

"Just watch," Jake said with a sly grin. Ricky knew that look – Jake was up to something.

Ricky kept his eyes on the house to see what Jake was talking about.

"Ah, there they are," Jake said, his grin getting bigger as he looked towards the back of the cabin.

Ricky followed his gaze and saw three squirrels spiraling up one of the columns of the porch towards the roof. Each squirrel hopped in a synchronized rhythm. When the first one stopped, the second and third also stopped with precision. When the lead began moving again, the second and third followed suit with fuzzy tails bouncing in coordinated patterns.

"What are they…?" Ricky started to ask.

"Shh…" Jake said, obviously enjoying what was about to happen.

The trio of squirrels made their way towards the chimney and satellite dish on the roof. The lead squirrel held up his paw to stop the others and looked around carefully to survey the area. After a moment, his head snapped forward and his paw gestured the others ahead. They all converged around the gray plastic satellite dish as if it were a witch about to be burned at the stake.

The lead squirrel gestured towards some black wires that connected to the mushroom shaped part of the dish that pointed towards the large bowl area. The other two squirrels descended on the wires and ravenously began to chew on them. Small bits of black plastic and silver strands of wire began to fly as they shredded the wire's coating and insulation.

About this time, Ricky noticed that the television sounds from inside the cabin began to warble and turn to static. Randall Woodman was starting to sit up and become visibly agitated.

The trio of squirrels finished their work on the coaxial cables and turned their attention to the dish itself. All three of them leapt onto the dish and started to rhythmically jump and pull at it in various directions. After a few moments, Ricky could see that the dish no longer pointed in the same direction it had just a short while ago.

At this point, Jake was chittering and laughing hysterically. Randall Woodman on the other hand, was not amused.

Randall threw the second of the metal cans at the television, which fell to the carpet and proceeded to release its remaining contents in a small puddle. Ricky thought he heard some of those unfamiliar words that Emma's Dad had said when fighting with the grill, but this human had a much harsher edge to his voice.

Ricky watched as Randall left the main room through one of the inside doors. A moment later he came back with a long black rifle in his hands.

"Oh crumbs," Ricky said to himself. "This doesn't look good at all."

Randall burst through the front door out onto the porch and down the front stairs.

Jake squealed a signal to the squirrel team on the roof, and they quickly jumped off of the dish.

"I'll kill every last one of you lousy tree rats!" Randall yelled as he raised the rifle towards the squirrels on the roof. All three heard him and paused for a moment. Human and squirrel eyes met briefly in a shared moment of animosity.

Randall trained the rifle on the squirrels and squeezed the trigger.

BANG!

Randall's shoulder recoiled with the rifle and he activated a lever on the side that caused a shiny brass cartridge to spin wildly out of the side of the weapon. *Ch-chick.* Smoke coiled from the barrel.

The squirrels bolted in a blur of fuzzy gray motion.

BANG! Ch-chick. BANG! Went the rifle.

More empty cartridges went flying. More smoke from a hot barrel.

The sound of the gun was startling and jolting each time. Ricky had to resist the urge to run or cower behind the log. Did he hit the squirrels? Did they make it out ok?

Behind the cabin he saw one squirrel run towards a large pine tree. It started to spiral its way up the safety of the backside.

A moment later, a second squirrel bolted from the back of the cabin and ran up an adjacent tree.

There was no third squirrel.

Randall made his way back towards the rear of the cabin, pulling that lever on the rifle that made the mechanical sound as another shell went flying out. He proceeded to assess the damage to the satellite dish on the roof.

"Damn squirrels," he said bitterly.

Ricky looked over at Jake and saw raw hatred there. "Did he just kill one of your...?"

At that moment, the third squirrel leapt from the roof right into the reddish hair of Randall Woodman.

The frenzy that ensued was chaotic. Randall dropped the rifle and clawed uselessly at his own head, hair, and face as the squirrel proceeded to run all over him like he was a burning tree stump.

Jake's demeanor perked up noticeably with this latest event, but Ricky was still in shock. "Get him!" Jake squeaked with wild eyes and closed squirrel fists.

The human-squirrel fight continued for a few brief but intense seconds. The squirrel made its way down through Randall's plaid shirt, which caused him to fall on the ground and flop around uselessly. His arms and legs flailed, trying to locate the furry intruder that was too fast to be caught.

Finally, the squirrel shot out of Randall's sleeve like a too-large pipe cleaner coming out of a narrow tube. It bolted towards one of the pine trees and launched itself about six feet up in a single leap.

It looked back towards the human just long enough for their eyes to meet. It then shook its tail a few times, chattered a bit, and disappeared around the backside of the trunk.

"Mission accomplished," Jake said triumphantly.

Ricky was stunned. "What the heck just happened? I'm pretty sure that was *not* the mission objective!"

"Not the original mission. Not your mission - the *wrong* mission. Our *new* mission. To foil this horrible human at every possible turn. He deserves every misery we can deliver and then some," Jake said. His expression was angry and bitter.

"Why? The mission is to *save* this man. Why have you taken it upon yourself to do this?" Ricky asked, perplexed at this open rebellion.

"Wait a few minutes and I'll show you what this terrible human is all about," Jake said.

Ricky really didn't know what to do, other than to let this play out and see what Jake's motivation was.

Randall brushed himself off angrily as he got up from the ground. He picked up his black rifle roughly and looked it over. He then raised it to his shoulder and took a couple of shots at the pine trees, even though the squirrels were long gone.

BANG! Ch-chick. BANG! Each one still made Ricky jump.

Randall then disappeared into the house for a few moments, only to return and jump into the pickup truck. He slammed the door shut and the engine fired up with a roar. Bits of gravel flew out from under the big tires as the truck took off nearly sideways.

"Good riddance," Jake said ruefully. "That should keep him away for a bit. Let's go."

Ricky followed Jake as he made his way down the slope towards the backside of the cabin. In the rear there was a screen door with a small silver latch keeping it closed.

"Would you like to do the honors?" Jake asked, eyeing Ricky's dexterous paws.

"Uh, sure," Ricky said. He then reached up and easily opened the latch. Raccoons have fabulously skilled paws for this sort of thing. The door swung open with the sound of a stretching metal spring. They both went inside, and Ricky closed the door gently behind them.

Looking around, Ricky could see that this was the kitchen. It was a mess. Plates, bowls, pots, and glasses were piled up in the sink and on the counters. There was a small table with two chairs haphazardly placed nearby. The faint odor of putrid food floated around in pockets of stale air that mixed with the smell of cedar.

Two large bowls for Rosco the dog were on the floor near the stove. The water bowl was about half-filled with a puddle on the floor completely encircling the entire area. The food bowl itself was empty, but Ricky could see a bunch of round brown nuggets that had rolled underneath the stove. Evidently the dog could only reach so far with his nose and tongue to get any runaways.

"Ok, so he's a bit of a slob, but that doesn't mean you should break protocol and ignore the mission orders," Ricky said, still puzzled about Jake's actions.

"Let's keep going," Jake said as he started his way out of the kitchen.

They passed the large white refrigerator as they went into the living room. The face of it was almost as messy as the kitchen itself. Magnets, notes, comics, and a few crudely drawn pictures. A faded photo of two men standing with rifles in the woods was stuck behind a large round magnet. One of the men was Randall, while the other looked similar, but was a fair amount older. There was also a large wooden cross and a few passages from the human's bible on little cards. A gold and black magnet said "U.S. ARMY RANGER" in large letters.

The refrigerator vibrated and emitted a droning hum that tickled Ricky's long whiskers. He was reminded briefly of the time travel accelerator chamber from far off in the future.

Ricky paused to inspect the largest of the drawings. It was a scene of three humans – a mother, a father, and a boy in the middle. There was also a small brown dog that looked like it could be a puppy. The three humans looked like potatoes with stick legs, but you could tell that they were holding hands and smiling. There were trees on the side and a yellow sun with straight lines beaming out of it like toothpicks stuck into a lemon.

It seemed like a very old drawing, as the edges were curled and the colors a bit faded. Ricky saw a bit of writing partially obscured in the lower left corner. He reached out and unfurled it to see what was there. The artist had signed the masterpiece: *Billy, Age 5.* He let the curl return slowly.

"Come on, let's go. He won't be gone forever," Jake said.

"Where did he go, anyway?" Ricky asked.

"Probably to the store to get replacement parts. And more beer no doubt."

Something suddenly occurred to Ricky and his eyes grew large in his furry face. "Wait a second… did you have anything to do with the barbecue grill at Emma's house?"

Jake smiled knowingly while peering back at Ricky from the side. "You're catching on my friend. These humans think they are so smart and sophisticated. That is, of course, until you take their primitive technology away or inconvenience them in the slightest. Then they resort to their base nature and stomp about like cavemen."

"I don't understand. Why would you sabotage Emma's

barbecue grill?" Ricky asked, now feeling a little uneasy and protective for his new friend.

"To get you out here alone, of course. Well, that and it fits into our general plan of revenge on all humans. Don't worry, we won't hurt you or your pink friend."

"I still don't…" Ricky started to say.

"Just keep moving and you'll see," Jake said.

They arrived in the center of the living room and stood on an old looking floor mat of dirty tan and blueish woven cloth. This room had a mustier smell that reminded Ricky of the human museum from his own time and the archives his parents used to store old artifacts in.

From this spot, they had a clear view into both the kitchen and the bedroom.

"Look around," Jake said while pointing towards the walls and shelves.

Ricky had thought that he and Jake were alone in the room, so was very startled to see that they were not. Animals of every kind were there – deer, foxes, squirrels, skunks, fishers, bobcats, rabbits, and even raccoons!

Jake saw the look of awe on Ricky's face and pointed towards the bedroom. "Don't forget her," he said.

Ricky turned and saw a large black bear in the corner. How had he not seen them?! Suddenly he felt so much more at ease. It was like being home with friends.

Only something wasn't right. They weren't moving.

"Um, are they playing around or something?" Ricky asked with a nervous chuckle.

Jake didn't answer, but Ricky saw the seriousness on his face.

Ricky moved a little closer to one of the raccoons nearby. It was perched on a small log with a furry paw outstretched in front. It was like a frozen statue, reaching for something.

Ricky circled around the front slowly. "Um, hello?" he said as he tried to look into its eyes. There was no response.

He reached out and touched one of the outstretched paws.

It was cold and felt like stone. Ricky pulled his own paw back like he had touched a hot flame.

Ricky's eyes grew wide and an expression of utter horror crept onto his face. He started moving backwards slowly but his gaze was still locked on the eyes of the frozen raccoon.

"Tell me this is not what I think it is," Ricky said quietly.

"I wish I could," Jake said. "But it's exactly what you think it is. They are all dead. Not just dead, mind you, but murdered. Trapped. Shot. Stabbed. Poisoned. Murdered in their homes, ripped apart to be eaten or thrown away, and what you see here is just the skin. Stretched over pieces of plastic as morbid trophies of who this man killed."

"It can't be…" Ricky started to say, tears welling up in his eyes.

"Oh, it is. This man is a hunter. That means he kills animals just for the sheer fun of it," Jake said with disgust.

Ricky was trying to keep his composure, but he was finding it increasingly difficult. He looked around at all of the different animals. He was starting to see that some of them were decapitated so that they could be mounted on the walls. Others were in unnatural poses to make them look ferocious. All had eerie blank stares looking out into nothingness. All of them were dead.

Everywhere he looked was another face, another life that was violently taken. He had flashes of days spent in the park with his friends back home. The sounds of the barred owls he would hear around the old neighborhood. The fox family from down the road. Mother, fathers, sons, and daughters. How could anyone do this for *fun*?

There were shelves that had just *parts* on them. The feet of rabbits. A jacket with a bit of fox fur around the neck. Shiny tan boots with the distinctive pattern of *skin*. He wasn't sure from what animal. There were also a bunch of fish mounted to small wooden plaques. A pile of fuzzy squirrel tails. Behind those he saw a hat made out of the skin and tail of a raccoon.

Ricky tried to fight back the tears that were now flowing, but it was no use.

He saw other raccoons grouped together behind the one he had touched. Two of them were young kits. What of their lives? What had they done to deserve this? Were these bigger raccoons even their parents, or were their parents left to mourn their dead children? Either way it was barbaric and too terrible to comprehend.

Through tears and sniffles, Ricky was trying to think about this rationally and objectively. "Even still, if the mission is to save this man, then…"

"He killed Isabelle," Jake said plainly.

It took a moment for this to really register. "Wh-what?" Ricky asked slowly through his shock. "You mean he hunted her? He shot her?" It occurred to him that Isabelle might actually be here as one of these horrible statues. He was suddenly afraid to look around and see her.

"No. At least these animals had some reason for their deaths, albeit sick and perverse. He just killed her like she was nothing and left her," Jake replied.

Jake's face was tightly knotted with the painful memory. "Come on. Let's get out of here and I'll tell you what happened. That foul dog might come back soon."

Ricky's desire to hear the story right now was tempered by his desire to leave this awful place. "Ok, let's go," he said as he turned his eyes back towards the floor.

They snaked back from the main room into the messy kitchen. It no longer seemed so bad in contrast to what they had just seen. He could only imagine what animal parts might be in the refrigerator. Ricky pushed open the back door and reset the latch to ensure their visit would not be noticed.

After turning around, Ricky saw Jake gesture towards the other building behind the cabin – the one with the active smokestack. "Take a quick look," Jake said.

Hesitantly, Ricky stretched up to peer through a small window. At first, he only saw a reflection of his own furry masked face, but as he shielded the glass from the sun with his paw and moved his nose closer to the glass, he could make out more of what was inside.

He saw the shape of a large gun rack with row after row of black and camouflage stocks. There were also racks of clothes. Some orange, some camouflage, some a greenish olive drab. Fishing supplies were in one corner. On a bench there were a bunch of tools, and a series of wicked looking metal traps. Some complicated looking bows occupied another area with barbed metal arrows nearby.

"I don't have the heart to take you in there," Jake said. "That's where he skins them and cuts them apart to be smoked or tanned."

Ricky also saw some brown boxes with shiny black lenses that looked like cameras of some kind.

Jake saw him looking at them. "Those are trail cameras. He uses them to find out where the animals go at night. He then puts down traps and waits for some poor creature to stumble upon them."

Ricky had no desire to see any more. He pulled back from the window and shook his head as if to clear the images from his mind. They both started walking towards the safety of the woods. Ricky noticed his leg hurting a little more as his pace quickened involuntarily.

They kept walking for a while until the cabin was completely out of site. Then they walked a bit more. They had left the pine grove and the sunlight was now visible in little dappled patches on green moss beneath the maples and oaks. Jake finally jumped up and perched on a tree stump in a small clearing.

Ricky knew this must have been incredibly difficult for Jake, but he had to know. "How did it happen?" he asked. "Isabelle, I mean."

Jake inhaled and exhaled slowly. "We had just arrived in this time and were scoping out each of the targets, just as planned."

Ricky sat down and rubbed his throbbing leg as Jake continued.

"We saw the butcher and were unsure of why we should save him, but we figured the directors and the coordinators must have had their reasons. We would do as we were instructed when the time came."

"So… why didn't you?" Ricky asked.

"Then we came here," Jake said without pause. "We saw what you just saw, but again we figured there must be a reason for it. So, we learned what we could about the target over the course of a few days."

Ricky was suddenly envious that Jake and Isabelle had enough time to really scope out the targets. His own experience seemed so rushed.

Jake continued. "On one day in particular, we were walking along the right side of that dirt road after spending the day gathering intel. We were both tired, so when we heard his truck coming, we didn't run away, but figured we would just stay on the side of the road and blend in like native squirrels."

Jake stopped the story at this point, and Ricky saw how sad his face looked. He had known Jake for a while, and he was always upbeat. Chipper. Energetic. Seeing him angry earlier on was unsettling, but now this seemed worse.

"We weren't even in the road," Jake said. "We were hopping on the grassy area – it's much softer on our paws."

Ricky saw Jake's expression change again. It was hard to place, but it seemed like a mix of utter shock and horror.

"The truck got closer and that dog started barking out of the window. Just as the truck was about to pass us, I looked to my left and saw it swerve *towards* us. Isabelle disappeared under one of those huge black tires, only to reappear a moment later – broken and bloody as she rolled to a stop in the grass.

The truck swerved back onto the road without even slowing down."

Ricky didn't know what to say. He could only imagine the horror of seeing such a thing happen to someone you love.

"There was nothing I could do. I didn't... I didn't even get to say goodbye," Jake said quietly.

Tears rolled down Jake's soft gray cheek as he looked off at the ground, as if thinking about what he would say to her if he had the chance.

"I carried her here and buried her myself," Jake said. He pointed to a small mound next to the stump and lowered his head into his paws.

Ricky didn't know what to say, but he remembered Monique comforting him earlier. He put his own paw gently on Jake's back.

After a few moments, Jake's face lifted and then turned hard again. "That's when I knew I couldn't continue with the mission as planned. They got it wrong! We were sent here to *help* animals, not to help those who would destroy them without so much as a second thought."

Seeing the look on Jake's face, Ricky recoiled his paw and took a step back.

"So, you are exacting revenge on this human... by taking out his satellite dish?" Ricky asked timidly.

"I'd kill him with my bare paws if I could!" Jake screeched with clenched fists. "But seeing as he's about a thousand times bigger than me, I've had to settle for what we can do."

"And the other squirrels?" Ricky asked.

"The squirrels of this time were more than happy to join the cause. Did you see the squirrel tails in that cabin? He's decimated the local population."

"But if you know he's a threat, can't you just tell everyone to avoid him?" Ricky asked.

"Most of the time it's the younger ones or those desperate for food. It's the same with the other animals, but many of them are too scared to act or even come close to this place," Jake said gesturing to the general area of the cabin. "We squirrels stand united."

"Maybe he could be reasoned with?" Ricky asked hesitantly. "He seems to be genuinely kind to that dog, Rosco."

"I know! Isn't that the most ridiculous thing?!" Jake asked incredulously. "He will trap, shoot, maim, and kill any animal that crosses his path, but at the same time he dotes on that dog."

"It does seem strange," Ricky said.

Jake continued. "He shares his food, he scratches his belly and pets him for hours, he throws that stupid yellow ball and plays with him every day. The dog is just as odious as he is – he hunts and kills us too. How can you love some animals and kill others?"

That struck a chord with Ricky – he had seen that same behavior in Emma. She was the sweetest human he knew, but she also was responsible for many deaths by eating the flesh of other killed animals. But he understood what she had said about being raised with that as the norm. All animals, humans included, tend to act however they are influenced to by their parents and those around.

"Maybe he just doesn't know any other way," Ricky said. "I saw a photo of him hunting with another human, probably his father. Maybe that was just how he was raised. If the mission is to save…"

"Look, I don't give a damn!" Jake said sharply. He hopped off of the wood stump and gave Ricky a harsh look from just a few inches away.

"This human is a monster and doesn't deserve to live. If he's going to die naturally, then so be it."

Jake looked over at the mound where Isabelle was buried. "I'll sleep better knowing he's gone. I sure as hell won't go out of my way to do *anything* to help him, let alone save his life. You shouldn't either," Jake said resolutely.

With that, Jake started to walk off into the woods. He turned around briefly to look back. "The humans don't *deserve* to be saved," he said emphatically. "Let them go extinct." It was pretty apparent that he didn't want to talk anymore, so Ricky let him leave.

Ricky was then left alone in the clearing to think about things. He kept finding his gaze falling onto the mound of earth that held the broken remains of Isabelle. He hobbled over and sat down next to her. He stretched out his paw and patted the ground gently.

"I'm sorry that this happened to you," he said. "You didn't deserve this."

They all knew that their mission was dangerous, but it seemed so senseless to travel through space and time for the betterment of the world, only to be carelessly killed by the one you were trying to help.

But was it really up to them? Maybe the directors knew what they were doing. Maybe by saving someone so terrible it might make a difference somehow. Ricky was having a hard time figuring out how that could be the case, but they had told him many times during training that he needed to *trust the mission*.

It might be difficult, but he needed to keep a clear head about this. He gave the grave another soft pat.

"I'm so sorry Isabelle, but I need to complete this mission. I hope I'm doing the right thing."

Ricky slowly hobbled back home. *The shed*, he had to remind himself. He was surprised how quickly it was starting to feel that way though.

CHAPTER TWELVE: *THE PICNIC*

*T*he picnic was in full swing by the time Ricky made it back. There were a number of humans milling about with floppy white plates loaded with food. A variety of savory smells hit his nose and he realized how long it had been since he had eaten.

As he limped towards the shed, he saw Monique peering out cheerfully from the darkened interior behind one of the doors. It was so good to see a friendly face.

"I was beginning to get worried!" Monique exclaimed with a smile.

Ricky hopped up into the shed and surprised Monique with a strong hug. She squeezed him back and he instantly felt much better.

"I'm sorry, it just took longer than I thought it would to scope out the next target," Ricky said.

"Well, I'm glad you're back. Are you hungry?" she asked.

"Famished. Is there anything that we can eat?"

"Of course! Sit down and rest that leg. I'll be back with a plate for you," Monique said as she walked towards the door.

"Uh, can you make sure that…" Ricky started, but Monique already knew what he was going to ask. "Yes, no meat for you. I've given it up too," she said with a smile.

"Thank you," Ricky said, feeling very grateful.

A little while later, Monique and Emma came into the shed, both carrying what seemed like a ridiculous amount of food.

"Soup's on!" Emma said as she sat, and they placed the various food items down around them on the wooden floor.

"Soup? I don't see any," Ricky said with confusion.

"Ah, that's just an expression. Never mind," Emma said. "Dig in!"

Ricky tore into dish after dish. It was as if he hadn't eaten in days. There were hard crunchy discs that Emma said were made out of corn and some stick-like things that were made from potatoes. They were so salty it made his lips pucker, but oh they were good!

Monique had a pool of bright red sauce that she dipped her potato sticks into. She called it "cats up" or something like that. For a moment Ricky was worried it might be cat blood or something, but Monique leaned in and said it was just made out of tomatoes. Weird. He tried some and it had a flavor that really complemented the salty potato sticks.

"Ooh, this is tangy! I like it," Ricky exclaimed as he tilted his head back and chomped away, his mouth alive with pops of flavor.

Emma had brought two bowls of water for each of them, and Monique showed him how she liked to dunk her bread in the cool water to get it nice and saturated. Ricky did the same and enjoyed every squishy bite. It was like getting that explosive gush of juice from fresh grapes. A raccoon's delight!

Emma then put a pile of white curly things on his plate, and said it was a "salad" of some kind. He had never seen a salad that looked like this before. There was a white sauce and a few chunks that he recognized as onions and bits of broccoli. He tried it carefully.

"Oh wow, this is really yummy!" he exclaimed.

Emma smiled proudly. "Made it myself. I even used vegan mayo for you."

"Vegan mayo?" Ricky asked with a little confusion.

"Yeah, it means that the white sauce doesn't have any animal ingredients in it," she replied.

"Ah, I appreciate that. Thank you!" he said with genuine

gratitude.

Ricky was starting to feel very full when Emma reached behind her back and produced one last plate as she opened her bright green eyes wide. "Dessert time!"

Ricky and Monique looked at each other with wide grins.

They proceeded to work through an assortment of cupcakes, cookies, and fruit pies. They were all amazing. Why did the humans choose to eat meat when they had so many other delicious options? This really was a puzzling time.

After a good long while of feasting, the three of them practically collapsed in a pile on the floor together. Ricky rolled himself over enough to see the other two. "Thank you for sharing that with me," he said, his whiskers twitching as he smacked his mouth and savored the last sweet tastes lingering there.

Emma rolled back towards him and she beamed a sweet smile. "Of course! That's what friends do." Monique nodded in agreement. Ricky felt so much gratitude for them both.

Emma then jumped up suddenly. "Ooh! Let's take a group photo!" She reached into her pocket and pulled out her phone. She took a few moments to set it up on a nearby box. She balanced it ever so carefully so that it was facing in the right direction.

Ricky hesitated, thinking it might be against protocol, but after a moment decided it would be worth whatever punishment they might hand him for such a minor infraction.

After starting some kind of timer on her phone, Emma sat in the middle and pulled both raccoons close to her. Monique on her right, and Ricky on her left. They bunched up together and smiled as the timer counted down. A beep and a flash of light let them know that the photo was complete.

Emma excitedly pulled the phone back and the three of them reviewed the photo together. Ricky felt himself choking up a little as he saw it. They looked so happy together – like three lifelong friends on an adventure. He never expected such a rollercoaster of emotions on this mission.

The happiness was somewhat fleeting though, as he remembered his mission and what had transpired that morning with Jake and the hunter.

Emma saw his expression change. "What's wrong?" she asked with a concerned tone.

Ricky didn't see any point in keeping them in the dark, so he told them everything. He told them about the hunter, the squirrels and the dish, about the frozen animal statues, about Jake and Isabelle, and about Jake's plea that he not complete the mission. It was a lot of serious stuff to lay on them all at once, but he felt better having shared it with them. How would they take it?

Emma seemed deep in thought when she finished. When she finally spoke, she held out her hand. Ricky saw the gesture and put his paw in it.

"That must have been horrible for you," she said gently.

"Yes, it was," he said sheepishly. He felt bad even telling them all of the details, but they were burned into his mind like a brand. Maybe they could help him share the load in a way.

"Why is it ok for people to hunt and kill innocent animals? Why do they do it?" Ricky asked in a curious but sad way.

Emma thought about it for a moment. "Most people today don't hunt themselves, but a lot of it is probably related to how humans are with food – we just grow up with that being the norm. It's not anything I would ever do in my life as it is, but if I were raised that way I might," she said.

"That's good that you don't hunt yourself," Ricky said earnestly. "But do many humans support the industry? Do you buy animal products like leather and fur?"

"I never really thought about it much before, but there are a lot of products that have animal skin in them, especially cow leather," Emma said as she looked down at her brown hiking boots and rubbed one slightly with her thumb. "It's everywhere – like car seats, jackets, shoes, belts, wallets, and a bunch of other things. It's actually hard to avoid sometimes."

"What about fur?"

"Well, I think that real fur is becoming less of a thing because some people speak out about how cruel it is."

"That's good that some humans are making a stand on behalf of the animals," Ricky said. "But why are cows any different from furry animals?"

Emma laughed to herself a little. "I guess it's really stupid, but some humans tend to protect the 'cute' animals more than the others. There are lots of folks who will speak out about seals and foxes and things, but less that will put themselves out there for a cow."

"That's kind of sad," Ricky said. "Why does a subjectively 'cute' animal deserve to live, and another deserve to die?"

"I honestly don't know," Emma said. "Humans just aren't that rational. It kinda relates to the entire human versus animal argument too."

"How do you mean?"

"Well, if you had an ugly human that wasn't that smart, would it be ok to eat them? I don't think so. But the same logic seems to apply to animals without a problem," Emma said wryly.

Ricky looked a little surprised at Emma's observation. "You're right! It really is like that. Humans seem to see themselves as 'superior' in some way and feel justified in killing others that are inferior."

"It's not limited to animals either, humans kill each other when they feel threatened, though not usually to eat. Sometimes I wonder if we really deserve to be saved," Emma said darkly as her gaze fell to the wooden floor.

She then raised her head and looked at Monique who was looking back with kind eyes. Seeing her furry face made Emma smile. "But I know there is good too. There is love and compassion in almost every human, even if it takes some effort to see it."

"I guess so," Ricky replied. "It's just hard to make the effort to save someone who seems so heartless about others. I hate to use the term, but so *evil*. I've been tasked with saving this man, but I'm not sure he deserves saving."

"You still have to complete your mission," Emma said determinedly. "If it will help animals in the future you have to do it. Plus, how can it be wrong to save a life?"

"Well," Ricky said, "just like the butcher, if this man continues to kill animals as he always has, I will share responsibility for their deaths."

"Maybe he will change. Your leaders or whatever must have sent you on this mission for a reason," Emma said.

"Jake is convinced that the mission is a mistake. And maybe he's right. Maybe someone hijacked the directives or something," Ricky said. "I'm still very conflicted about it, but I have to think that you are right. Maybe I just can't see the same big picture that the directors do. I keep telling myself I should trust in the mission."

Ricky really wasn't sure if that was the right thing to do, but he had to make a choice. If he listened to Jake and didn't save the hunter, he would be sabotaging the mission and all that it stood for.

"Monique, what do you think?" Ricky asked. She had been quiet this entire time.

"So… you're saying a bunch of rogue squirrels sabotaged her dad's grill just to get you away from us?" she asked. Ricky wasn't sure what he expected Monique to say, but for some reason that wasn't it.

"Um, yes," he replied.

"How do you know you can trust anything this Jake character is saying?" Monique asked. She seemed to be getting a little defensive.

"Honestly I don't know. He definitely believes that what he is doing now, taking revenge on the humans, is the right thing to do," Ricky replied.

"But he might be blinded by grief," Monique said calmly. "I think you need to save whomever you can whenever you can. That's the right thing to do."

Ricky was still conflicted but found himself smiling. Somehow it was impossible to argue with the purity of Monique's assessment.

Ricky took a moment to think about the responses from both of them. He ran his paws on the rough wooden floor and looked at the bright sunlight through the window. The birds were chirping away at a dozen happy songs. Somehow that made the decision easier.

"Ok," Ricky said looking back and forth between them. "I'll stick to the plan. Thank you both for your input."

"Of course," Emma said. Monique nodded in agreement. It was good to have support with such a difficult decision.

Tomorrow he would carry out the mission as planned.

That night, Ricky kept waking up, expecting Minka to visit at any moment and drop some searing wisdom on him that would put everything into doubt. But the shed remained quiet.

He wasn't sure if that was a good thing or a bad thing.

CHAPTER THIRTEEN: *R. WOODMAN*

*R*andall Woodman was going through his regular routine as Ricky watched from a safe distance on the hill. He had gotten there very early in order to ensure he was there in plenty of time. Rosco the dog was nowhere to be seen, so it was just Ricky and Randall.

He still didn't know how Randall was going to die and how he should intervene, so he played a little game with himself. Could he figure out what was going to happen?

Randall was working on his big gray truck at one point, and he had jacked it up to access the underside. He drained a bunch of black liquid out into a pan. Ricky wondered if that was oil of some kind for the internal combustion engine.

He chuckled to himself as he thought about what he was seeing. It seemed so silly that the humans thought they could endlessly use and burn the fossilized remains of other dead inhabitants of earth without consequences. Oh, the irony!

But back to the task at hand. Maybe the truck would fall on him? Ricky had no idea how he would successfully intervene if that were the case, but Randall finished whatever work he was doing underneath the truck without incident. He then lowered the truck back down and poured some new amber colored liquid in the top. He closed the front flap of the truck with a loud bang. Scratch that one off the list.

He then got a bright red plastic container and seemed to be pouring another liquid into a different hole in the side of the truck. Ricky thought about it and concluded it was probably gasoline. He knew that gasoline was another substance derived from Earth fossils and was in dwindling supply at this time. It was extremely flammable, explosive, and caused cancer if you breathed in the fumes.

Randall dying instantly from cancer seemed unlikely, but maybe the gasoline would ignite by accident? Ricky watched as Randall emptied the container, set it back down on the ground and put a silver cap over the hole in the truck without incident. No luck on that guess.

Later on, Randall was sitting on the porch cleaning one of his guns with a splotchy rag and some more oil. They used that stuff for everything! Ricky prepared himself to run in and push the gun away if that was what Randall was doing at the appointed time. But the gun cleaning came and went without any problems.

Ricky kept a close eye on his wristband to watch the countdown to the specific time that he was supposed to act. It was getting closer and closer. The coordinates were off slightly from his present location, but from his visit with Jake he knew that this was the target. As long as he followed Randall's movements he would be in the right place at the right time. It was just a question of the "intervening" that would be needed.

A little later, Randall wheeled out a large orange machine from behind the cabin. He spent some time getting it running, but once he did it made an incredibly loud sound as some internal mechanisms spun round and round. Randall picked up some large branches from the area around the cabin and fed them into the noisy machine.

It chewed them up like they were bits of nothing and spat out small chunks of wood from a chute on the other side. This was definitely a machine that could kill someone easily if they made a wrong move. Maybe one of the branches would catch on his clothing and he would be pulled in and ground up? Jake would be thrilled, but Ricky didn't think he could stand to see something like that happen. He would have to switch the machine off or maybe trip Randall before he made the fatal error.

But, alas, the wood chewing process came and went.

"Come on!" Ricky said, and then immediately felt bad about having said it. He giggled a little to himself though.

Randall finally went inside and started to look in the refrigerator for dinner. He pulled out a small plastic dish and lifted up a corner of the red rubbery lid to take a look inside. He got close to take a sniff. He must not have smelled anything, because he got even closer and sniffed again. Ricky couldn't tell what it was, but it looked like chunks of brown and pink meat floating in some kind of brownish liquid. He could only imagine what animal gave its life for that. Maybe he would be poisoned? Or maybe he would eat too quickly and choke on a large chunk of it?

Ricky watched intently as Randall heated up the food in a glowing metal box that spun the dish around and around. Finally, the light shut off and a small bell let out a loud *ding* to signal the end of the cooking process.

Ricky checked the countdown timer on his wristband and saw that the appointed time was just minutes away.

This must be it!

If it were poisoning, then they would have sent him with some nano drones. So, it must be choking. He limbered himself up to get ready to bounce on Randall's diaphragm when it would happen. He stretched his raccoon legs and even gave his striped tail a quick primping.

Randall had taken the dish out of the metal box and sat at the small kitchen table. He dug at the dark and pink bits with a fork and knife and ate ravenously. Brown liquid dripped down from his mouth and covered the table around the dish. Ricky tried not to think about whatever animal had died for this meal to happen. What body part was he consuming? Did he even taste what he was eating? Did he appreciate the life he had ended? He didn't think so.

Randall continued to eat until the large chunks were gone.

There were a few white bits that he ate as well. Maybe potatoes? Or were they bits of fat? He didn't want to think about it.

Finally, he lifted the entire dish up into the air and poured the remaining brownish liquid into his mouth. Some dribbled down his chin as he did this. Ricky tried to quell his gag reflex while watching all of this. He was only partially successful.

Ricky kept checking the countdown. The time was almost upon them. He got ready to run into the kitchen and do whatever he needed to do. Fortunately, he had already opened the door latch once before, so he knew he would be able to open it again quickly.

The bright blue numbers on his wristband counted down rhythmically.

10 seconds to go.

Ricky got himself ready to pounce as soon as he could see the cause of death.

5 seconds to go. 4... 3... he was ready for whatever was about to happen.

He crouched down like a loaded spring about to release.

2 seconds... 1 second... and 0.

The display on the wristband started flashing red with the words "INTERVENE NOW!" in large bright letters.

Ricky thought that he was ready for anything that could have happened, only he wasn't. The reason being... that nothing happened.

Randall Woodman put the dish back down on the table and proceeded to burp loudly. He wiped his mouth with the back of his sleeve and got up from the table. He tossed the plastic dish into the sink and grabbed a beer from the refrigerator. He then plopped down on the big chair in the living room and turned the TV on with the remote. Randall Woodman was fine. Well, he was terrible, but he wasn't dying.

"Huh? I don't understand." Ricky said to himself. He checked the countdown timer on his wristband. It was now counting up from the point of intervention, with the large letters still flashing at him.

Ricky was very confused at this point. Why had nothing happened? He kept checking back on Randall, but it became more and more evident that he wasn't about to die. It was just another ordinary night in the cabin. Beer and TV. Belching and snoring.

Reluctantly, Ricky finally decided that he should head back to the shed. Maybe there had been some mistake in the mission details? Or maybe some other actions that he had taken had already stopped this historical event from happening? Maybe Jake interacting with the target had changed things just enough for this death to be avoided? He didn't know. He might have to talk to Jake again and see what he thought.

Ricky slowly made his way back to the shed on his sore leg. He hadn't got very far though, when he heard something coming towards him. The proximity alarm on his wristband gave him a squeeze to let him know it wasn't just the wind.

As the noise got closer, he was apprehensive about who or what it could be, so he was relieved when he saw it was a raccoon. Not just any raccoon, but Monique! What was she doing out here?

"Ricky, come quick!" she exclaimed, running towards Ricky with a concerned look on her face. A feeling of panic surged through Ricky.

"What is it? Are you ok?" he said frantically.

"Yes, I'm fine, but someone else is in trouble."

"Is it Emma?" Ricky asked with concern.

"No, it's a dog. He's caught in a metal trap in the woods,"

Monique replied. "My friend Hop-Hop told me."

They started running together in the direction that Monique was indicating.

"Hop-Hop?" Ricky asked.

"He's a crow," Monique said as she ran. "Friendly chap. Always looking out for others. He heard a yelping and whining sound and found this poor dog caught in a hunter's trap."

One of Randall Woodman's traps, no doubt. Were there any animals he didn't kill?

As they got closer to the location that Monique was leading them towards, Ricky took a moment to look at his wristband. It was still flashing "INTERVENE NOW!" as it was before. But this time Ricky was paying more attention to the GPS coordinates. He tapped them on the screen, and it showed a map of his current location, as well as the location of the target.

They were moving towards it!

"Here he is," Monique said as they pushed through some brush to enter a small clearing. There was a brown dog with its right front paw and leg locked into a large metal trap. There was a pool of bright red blood mixing in the dirt and the dog was whining in pain.

Ricky knew right away that it was Rosco, Randall Woodman's canine companion. He checked the coordinates on his wristband, and they matched exactly. This was the target! It was *Rosco* Woodman, not Randall Woodman that he needed to save!

"Damn, do they charge by the letter or something?!" Ricky asked irately. It would have been very helpful to have just a *bit* more information on the target. He hoped it wasn't too late. If he had been here on time, it probably would have been a simple matter of turning him away from the trap, but because he missed the appointment this would be much more difficult.

Ricky and Monique ran towards Rosco, but as soon as they got close, they had to stop and back off. Rosco was obviously in pain and not receptive to any help.

"Get away from me!" Rosco barked. He writhed in pain as

he said this and he seemed loath to let anyone near.

Ricky noticed a crow jumping around from branch to branch in a nearby tree. That must have been Hop-Hop.

"We are here to help you," Monique said as she stepped carefully closer.

"BARK BARK BARK BARK!" was the loud reply from Rosco. "Don't you dare touch me!"

He pulled at the trap and chain that was attached to the nearby tree trunk. Blood gushed from the wound on his leg with every motion. He let out a little whimper and his own weight collapsed him down to the ground.

"Why does he not want us to help him?" Ricky asked.

"He sees us as the enemy," Monique said. "He hunts and kills us, just like his human – that Randall person you were telling us about."

Ricky looked at the trap that was clamped onto Rosco's leg – it was made out black metal and had very large and substantial teeth. Maybe it was something for a bear or other large animal. What would happen once an animal got trapped in this? Were they just left to die from dehydration and blood loss over a period of hours or days? It was unfathomable that this level of suffering was acceptable to humans. Ricky fought back the urge to just leave.

"Even if we get close to him, I'm not sure that we can open that trap with just the two of us," Ricky said. "We are going to need help. Is there anyone that you can bring?"

Monique didn't hesitate. "Yes! It will take some time, but I will reach out to anyone that I can. Hop-Hop, get whomever you can as well!" she yelled in the crow's direction. Hop-Hop let out a loud "CAW!" and flew off in a flash of black feathers.

"I'm afraid I won't be much good to you," Ricky said. "I'll stay here with Rosco and see if I can help him to hang in there."

Monique nodded quickly and ran off into the woods. Ricky was now left alone with the *real* R. Woodman. With Monique and the crow gone, Rosco seemed to relax a little.

"How did you get caught in this trap?" Ricky asked, trying

to establish some rapport.

Rosco didn't answer.

"Is there anything I can do to make you more comfortable?" Ricky asked. Once he heard himself, he realized what a silly thing that was to ask, but he didn't know what else he could do.

Rosco lifted his head up slightly and looked in Ricky's direction. "You can go away trash panda and leave me alone." He relaxed his head back down partly on the trap and on his own injured leg. He winced with the pain.

"I have some medical training," Ricky said, hoping to keep the conversation going somehow. "I can see that you are losing a lot of blood, and you will probably pass out soon due to hypovolemic shock. Without treatment you will die very soon."

Rosco's expression changed a little as he started to realize the severity and truth of what Ricky was saying. He could feel his grasp on consciousness getting fuzzy. Ricky thought he heard him whimpering faintly with each ragged breath.

"I can help you if you let me," Ricky pleaded as he took a few careful steps forward. "We need to stop your blood loss until we can get you out of that thing."

Each small step towards Rosco was a small victory for the mission, but also brought Ricky closer to the freely moving and very sharp teeth of his target.

As Ricky moved closer, he started to unwrap his own injured leg. Without any other resources around, the long cloth bandage from the vet would have to do.

Step, unwrap. Step, unwrap.

There was a smooth metal splint that he pulled out once it became loose enough, and he discarded it in the grass that was still wet with morning dew. He could feel the warm air on his leg for the first time in a few days. It felt nice, but also a little disconcerting. His leg wasn't really healed yet, so it felt much less stable without the support of the bandage and splint. He stepped gingerly on the tender leg as he finally got within reach of Rosco.

He held the bandage up for Rosco to see. "I'm just going

to put some pressure on the wound to try to stop some of the bleeding. It will hurt, but it's the only way to save you."

Rosco looked at the bandage and also at Ricky's own matted and injured leg. Maybe Ricky's vulnerability is what finally helped to convince him that he wasn't the enemy. Or maybe he just felt more pain now and wanted it to be over. Either way, Rosco finally nodded to Ricky and relaxed enough for him to get in close.

Ricky moved quickly and with skilled paws. He weaved the long bandage around and around the leg of Rosco where he could. There was a lot of blood that matted the fur and the trap was in the way, but at least it would be something. He tried to save the cinching of the bandage for last, so that it would be a quicker and one-time process.

"Are you ready for the hard part?" Ricky asked.

Rosco closed his eyes and nodded.

Ricky pulled the bandage tight.

"YIPE!" Rosco yelped in pain and involuntarily clenched his entire body. The chain of the trap jingled as it shook.

"It's ok – just relax now. The worst is over," Ricky said. Rosco haltingly began to release his muscles again. Ricky then kept his paws on the wound to maintain steady pressure on it.

Ricky wanted to keep Rosco awake and conscious. "Hang in there Rosco, help is on the way. We'll get you out of there soon."

Rosco started mumbling softly without lifting his head. "How… how did you know my name?"

Ricky didn't want to reveal how he really knew his name, so he replied "my friend lives nearby and told me. Are you ready to tell me how you got in this trap?"

"I was running affterr a… rrrmmm… and… aarrmmm…" Rosco then passed out.

"Oh crumbs," Ricky said.

He could still feel Rosco's pulse, but it was getting fainter. There was nothing else to do but wait for reinforcements.

After what seemed like an eternity, Ricky's wristband gave a squeeze and he heard some rustling from the underbrush fast approaching. He squinted into the morning sun to see what was causing the disturbance.

It was Monique! And she had backup!

"Thank goodness you are here!" he yelled to her over the shortening distance between them. "I tried to stop the bleeding as best as I could, but he's already passed out. He won't have long."

"I brought some friends! I just hope it's enough," she yelled back as she bounced through the tall grass. Along with Monique came running a menagerie of different animals. There was a small deer, an opossum, a groundhog, and even a squirrel. Ricky couldn't tell if it was one of Jake's recruits, but was guessing it wasn't, given their hatred for the Woodmans.

They all came running together and coalesced quickly around Rosco and Ricky. Fuzzy paws started to feel around and pull at the trap in various directions. The deer held its hoof on the lower portion to hold it steady whilst the others pulled upwards against the heavy spring.

"I'm sorry we don't have time for pleasantries, but guys, this is Ricky," Monique said to the assembled group.

"Thank you all for coming," Ricky said as he gave a quick nod of hello to all. In turn they began to say hello back and introduce themselves amid the grunts and strains of pulling at the trap.

"Robert here," said the possum. He gave a little salute with his paw.

"Jesse," from the deer. She still had white spots and sounded pretty young.

"Chuck, at your service!" from the groundhog. He had a gruff but friendly voice.

"Jake," said the squirrel.

Ricky did a double take. "Wait, what? Your name is Jake too?"

The squirrel didn't seem phased. "Oh, you know another Jake? Yeah, it's pretty common amongst us squirrels. I have two brothers named Jake too. Mom and Dad weren't very creative with names. They liked to stay focused on foraging at all times."

"Oh," Ricky said. Squirrels had their own ways that you just had to accept.

Ricky was glad to have met everyone, but the grim reality of the situation was weighing heavily on him… Rosco was still out, and they were barely budging the trap.

With Jesse holding the bottom of the trap, Ricky and Monique were pulling at the top of the trap on one side, while Chuck and Robert pulled at the other side. The "other" Jake was in the middle, trying to slide Rosco's paw out. It wasn't moving and the motion of them working on the trap only seemed to be making the wound worse. The bandage that Ricky had put on was saturated with blood.

"I don't think this is going to be enough," Ricky said sadly. It seemed that the others had come to the same conclusion. They started to release their grips on the trap and let it sink to the ground. Rosco's leg fell with it. If the trap weren't attached to the tree with a chain, they could have just carried Rosco, but the hunter needed to make sure that whatever animal he trapped wouldn't be able to get away. It was cruel and effective.

Ricky had heard of trapped animals actually chewing off their own limbs in order to escape such a torture. Maybe if they had started earlier that could have been an option, albeit a horrible one. But Rosco had lost too much blood as it was. The only way to save him would be to get more muscle on the trap to open up those metal jaws enough to slide his leg out.

Ricky wasn't ready to give up yet though. "Think, think, think..." he said to himself. How could they pull apart such a strong device? There weren't any tools around, and the metal spring was crushingly powerful. Maybe if it weren't metal, he could…

"Wait!" he exclaimed aloud. "I've got it!" he said as his face lit up with hope.

He spread his arms out wide and started searching all around in the tall grass. The others had puzzled looks on their faces.

"Ah… if you are looking for a rock with which to hit the dog and put him out of his misery, I don't think that's a very good answer." Chuck said dryly. "Is he ok?" he asked Monique. She shrugged her shoulders. She had no idea what Ricky was up to either.

"Here it is!!" Ricky said as he held up a long shiny piece of metal that he had picked up from the grass. He hurriedly carried it over towards the trap. "It's the metal splint from my leg! It's light but incredibly strong. We can use it as a lever to pry the trap open!"

The other furry faces lit up with understanding. As a group they began to pull and strain at the metal trap once more. This time with the metal splint putting physics on their side.

"It's starting to work!" Ricky yelled. The trap's dark teeth were finally starting to move apart. But their muscles were starting to get fatigued, and the teeth were buried deep into the flesh and bone of Rosco's leg.

No, they couldn't have come this far just to fail now!

Ricky's arms were starting to shake from the effort. His wrist was almost vibrating too. Wait, that was his wristband's proximity alarm!

"CAW!"

Ricky looked up to see Hop-Hop landing on one of the branches above.

"I found these guys behind the butcher shop!" Hop-Hop screeched from a distance. What was he talking about?

A moment later, Ricky saw it. There were four large raccoons running at full speed across the clearing. They looked like fuzzy brown and black striped beach balls bouncing through the thick grass and wildflowers at an incredible pace.

"We're coming!" they yelled. Ricky couldn't tell which

one had said that, but it didn't matter. In mere seconds, they converged around Rosco and the trap. They were breathing heavily but had fresh muscles to lend to the cause. They were the biggest raccoons that Ricky had ever seen.

All but Ricky from the first crew backed out to let the new raccoons into place.

"Paws at the ready!" one yelled. "Now!"

Ricky leaned into the splint metal as the other four pushed and pulled on the iron jaws. It was working!

"Slide his paw out!" Ricky yelled. Robert the possum grabbed onto it with both of his front paws and heaved it clear of the trap.

"Ok, it's out!" Robert yelled.

The group released the trap all at once. It snapped back shut with a frightfully loud noise. It was so loud that all of them recoiled from the metallic clang that rang out across the field. Ricky's metal splint had spun into the jaws when he had let go of it, and it was now mangled inside the trap instead of Rosco's leg.

"You did it!" Monique said joyously as they all shared a moment of elation. "Now what?"

Ricky looked at the unconscious dog. "Now we can move him. We might be able to…"

BANG!

Ricky recognized that sound all too well. It was a gun from the other side of the field where the raccoons had come from. He took a moment to look across the field and confirmed what he had expected - it was Randall Woodman, come to look for Rosco.

"You furry bastards leave my dog alone!" he shouted angrily while sprinting towards them.

"Run!" Ricky screamed. Everyone scattered in an explosion of motion in different directions.

Randall paused in his running just long enough to take

another shot.

BANG!

Ricky thought he heard the sound of something hitting the ground behind him. "Keep going!" Monique yelled from his side as they ran.

They were just about to the tree line. She could have been faster on her own, but she was trying to help Ricky to run with his injured leg. "Maybe once he reaches Rosco he'll let us go," she said breathlessly.

Monique risked a look backwards as Randall made it to the area where Rosco was lying near the trap and the tree.

"What have you done to him?!" Randall screamed. He was kneeling down next to Rosco's unconscious body and must have seen all of the blood. He took aim and fired one more shot in their direction.

BANG!

Almost immediately, Ricky felt Monique trip and fall next to him. Only she didn't simply fall, she was hit.

"Noo!" Ricky shrieked as Monique crumpled and rolled next to him. The next few moments were a frenzy as Ricky tried to ascertain her condition. Maybe she was just grazed? No, she was holding her left paw to her face and there was blood streaming down her fur.

"Oh, Monique. No, no, no!" He felt himself fall to pieces as much as if he had been hit himself. He was suddenly reminded of Jake and Isabelle. Was this how it felt?

He had to suppress the urge to run back in a blind fury at Randall Woodman. At that moment he didn't even care if he survived the attempt. He grit his teeth and tried to focus on her.

"Monique, can you hear me? Are you ok?" he asked. He cursed himself for asking such a stupid question, but he didn't know what else to say.

"I don't know," she replied with a shaky voice. "My face hurts and I can't… I can't see anything out of my left eye." At least she was alive and conscious.

"Can you keep going? We aren't into the woods yet," Ricky said as he looked towards the nearby tree line.

"Yes, I think so," Monique said. "Ricky?" she asked timidly.

"Yes?"

"I'm so sorry. Maybe you should go on without me," she said sweetly.

"Monique… I wouldn't leave you behind for anything," he said, and he meant it.

"Come on, let's do this together," he said as he put his paws under her and tried to support some of her weight.

Their furry legs moved in unison as they stepped together and started to make some progress towards the safety of the woods. How the tables had turned! His leg burned with pain, but he didn't care.

They continued their slow trek into the cover of ferns and mossy trunks. Randall must have been occupied with Rosco, as he didn't pursue them any further.

They had made it.

The rest of the way back to the shed was technically the same distance as it was before, but for Ricky it seemed like the longest hike he had ever taken. Eventually they made it back and Ricky was able to find Emma to get Monique to the emergency vet.

He watched Emma and her father wrap her up in a blanket and put her in their car. As the red lights of the silent car grew smaller and went out of sight over a hill, Ricky slowly limped to the shed and collapsed into his bed, his face wet with tears for his friend.

CHAPTER FOURTEEN: *UPDATE*

*L*ater that evening, Emma came by to console Ricky and give him the latest update.

"She's going to be ok," she said as she sat down next to Ricky's bed on the wood floor. She suddenly recalled her dad coming to talk to her about Mom all those years ago and being in that hospital waiting room. Being the messenger wasn't any easier.

"Fortunately, they were able to remove all of the buckshot. The vet said she was lucky it wasn't a rifle round," she said.

Ricky breathed a sigh of relief and rubbed his face in his paws.

"Her eye?" he asked.

Emma looked away towards Monique's empty bed. "Unfortunately, she will most likely never see out of it again. But she still has vision on the right side, and she wasn't hit anywhere else."

He felt relief that she would make it through, but the injury to her face and loss of her eye was terrible. She didn't deserve that.

Emma handed Ricky a small package with a fresh bandage for his own leg, as well as a new metal splint. "These are for you. Let me know if you want any help putting it on."

"Ok, thanks," he said.

"Get some rest and we can figure things out in the morning. Don't worry, she's in good hands," she said, putting her hand around him and scratching the soft fur behind his ears.

Ricky nodded, still looking towards the floor. Emma leaned over and gave him a hug.

"Thanks Emma. Good night."

"Good night, Ricky," she said as she gave a little wave and closed the door to the shed.

Ricky took his turn to look over at Monique's empty bed and he felt himself choke up again. He got into his own bed and cried a bit more. Eventually exhaustion took over and he succumbed to sleep for the night.

CHAPTER FIFTEEN: *MIDNIGHT CHAT*

Ricky awoke to the proximity alarm on his wristband giving a slight squeeze. He put his paws over his face.

"Oh, no. Not tonight," he said. "Leave me alone!" he said to the darkness.

The darkness replied with Minka's voice. "I heard all about your adventures today with the hunter and his mutt."

"I'm seriously not in the mood for a midnight chat with you," he said plainly.

"That's nice," she replied, and then kept going. "Do you see now why your friend the squirrel is right? The humans are what they are. You can't change them."

She moved into a sliver of moonlight that only partially illuminated her face. It made her look mysterious and menacing. "They don't even *need* to hunt, but they do anyway. Don't get me wrong, I get it – hunting is fun. I do it all the time. I don't have to do it either, but I like to. It's in our DNA."

"This is fascinating. Thank you so much for your incredible insight," Ricky said sarcastically. This was really getting tiring.

"Anyway, have you checked out your third and final target yet?" Minka asked.

Ricky hadn't even thought much about that. "No, not yet."

"You aren't going to like it," she said in a mocking sing-song voice.

Ricky's commitment to the mission was hanging by a thread at this point. But he knew he should at least scope things out and make the decision for himself. Maybe this one would be different. He could hope.

"Good night, trash panda," she said teasingly.

Ricky didn't reply.

CHAPTER SIXTEEN: *TRAIL CAM*

Randall Woodman watched the video recording from the trail camera for a third time. Then again, a fourth time. His brain recognized what he was seeing, but he knew that it just wasn't possible.

He scrubbed through it on his computer in slow motion and frame by frame. He saw Rosco running from the right side of the screen towards the left. That looked normal. Then the trap sprung. Rosco always avoided those, but he must have been distracted. Randall flinched as he saw his beloved dog spin and flail in pain in the clutches of the trap.

Then came the bizarre part... the part that he kept watching again and again. The part that shook him to his very core.

"They saved him," he said to himself.

"They saved him."

PART FOUR: THE SCIENTIST

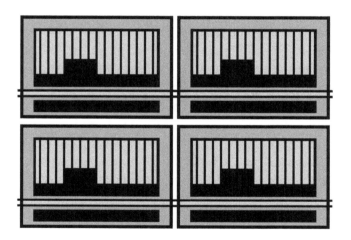

CHAPTER SEVENTEEN: *DR. K. NOVA*

Dr. Katie Nova was working with the new lab intern. She wasn't quite up to speed yet, but everyone had to start somewhere. As they walked down the rows and rows of animal cages, the intern took small breaks from chewing her gum to keep asking impertinent questions.

"Aww… the beagle puppies are so cute! Is it ok if I come over on my lunch break to play with them?" she asked with a chipper voice.

"Absolutely not," Dr. Nova replied sternly. "These animals are not pets. They shouldn't be bothered in any way. Feed them and give them water. Clean the cages. That's it."

"But, can't I at least just pet them a little?" the intern asked innocently.

"No. That will just upset them," Dr. Nova replied. "These animals are used to a routine. Petting them and causing a fuss over them just upsets them and makes them unhappy." These interns were so naïve.

"If you *do* pet one of them, they will have to be removed from the experiment, and who knows if the corporate office will allocate the funds for a replacement," Dr. Nova said as she stopped walking to face the intern directly. "The same goes for the kittens, the monkeys, the rats, and every other animal in here. You need to think about them like they are pieces of lab equipment. That's what they are. Got it?"

"Got it," the intern replied. She seemed to take the rebuke

in stride, continuing to chew her gum after a brief moment of silence. She also made a funny face and waved at the nearest cage of white mice when Dr. Nova wasn't looking.

"Do you ever get those crazy animal activists coming around here?" she asked as they continued walking.

Dr. Nova exhaled loudly. "No, fortunately very few people even know we are out here. That's why we've had to move our facilities so often to more remote locations."

The so-called animal rights activists were a serious pain. They were always going on about saving the animals from experiments, not knowing that some of those experiments might one day save them from dying of cancer or Alzheimer's disease.

The intern was looking at one of the gray tabby kittens that was curled up in a fuzzy ball. "They say there are other ways to do experiments that don't involve animals. Are they right?"

Dr. Nova looked as if she were insulted to be asked such a question. "Those methods are more expensive. Animals are cheap. And so is the corporate entity that just bought out this lab."

She didn't say it, but they would both be lucky if they still had jobs in the next year. The hours kept getting longer and the pay kept going down.

Dr. Nova snapped her fingers to pull the intern away from the cat. "Besides, half of those activists would show up wearing leather shoes and chow down on chicken wings without a second thought. Hypocrites."

After passing the last rows of primate cages and some computer servers, they entered Dr. Nova's office. It was cluttered but organized, with large academic books of every kind on a multitude of shelves. Large glass windows gave her a clear view down the middle of the cage rows. She sat behind her computer and dismissed the intern.

"Be back here Monday morning at 5:30AM for the first feeding shift," she said dryly. She would be surprised if this one lasted a month.

"Yes, Ma'am," the intern replied. She snapped her gum and spun around to leave.

Dr. Nova took a moment to organize some of the paperwork from the latest shipment of rats. They were called "Long-Evans" rats, which have a white furry body with a black hood that trails to a long black stripe down their back. Sometimes the accent color was tan, but usually they seemed to get the black ones. In pet stores they called them "fancy rats", but here they were just good ol' lab rats.

This latest shipment was supposed to have only two female rats for a small study's control group, but for some reason the delivery cage had *twenty-two* rats in it. Sometimes that happened if the breeders got sloppy. The females would come in pregnant and give birth en route. In this case, each female had eleven tiny fuzzy babies.

She took a sip of coffee from one of her many mugs on her desk and made a sour face at the bitterness of it. "Uck!" she exclaimed. Two weeks at the most for that intern.

She had put the mug down and was looking over the paperwork details when her phone rang. She picked it up casually.

"Dr. Katie Nova, animal research lab four," she said as she pushed her glasses up on her nose and sat back in her squeaky desk chair.

"Oh, hey Reggie. Yes, I was just looking that over. Looks like they will have twenty extra rats as backups for the study," she said.

She organized some of the paperwork as she listened to the person on the other end.

Her expression changed quickly after hearing something unpleasant. "Are you serious? They cancelled the experiment? Great," she said sarcastically.

"Well, no I won't have any other use for Long-Evans rats until next year. We are still working off of that last set."

She took off her glasses now and set them on her desk. She

scrunched up her forehead and rubbed it with her free hand.

"Yup, well they will have to get euthanized then," she said coldly. "I'm only paying for *two* rats though. I don't want to have to pay for two dead rats, so I'm sure as hell not going to pay for twenty-two dead rats."

She put the phone on her shoulder and started to loosen up her long black hair that was pulled back in a neat braid.

"Yeah, I know that tomorrow is Saturday. And no, for the last time I will not have dinner with you," she said with a sly smile.

"Yes, yes, I know I'm your 'geek goddess'. Flattery won't get you anywhere. Save it for your comic book convention this weekend."

She picked up one of her pens and rolled it around in her fingers. "Uh-huh. Maybe you'll find someone there who will put up with you. *Goodbye* Reggie," she said as she hung up the phone and gave a little smirk with a muted laugh.

A moment later her face turned more serious as she gave the paperwork one more look. She tossed the papers down on the desk. "What a great way to end the week," she said with disdain. "Looks like I'll be coming in tomorrow to sort this mess out."

She shut down her computer, grabbed her lab coat from the back of the chair, and walked out of her office. She walked past cage after cage of research animals. It was best not to look at them unless you had to. At the far end of the room, she clicked off the fluorescent lights to the lab and exited to one of the main hallways of the facility.

"Another fun day at the office," she said to herself.

CHAPTER EIGHTEEN: *THE DECISION*

Ricky really had wished that Jake and Minka were wrong about the third target. It would have been so much easier to find out how great this third person was and feel good about saving them. But no such luck.

Ricky was shimmying his way through a large air duct in the ceiling of the animal laboratory facility on reconnaissance when the sad truth hit him – they were right.

He had just worked through a multitude of different rooms in the building, and each one seemed worse than the last. He recalled his shock at being in the meat cooler at the butcher shop, and then his horror at seeing the frozen animal statues in the hunter's cabin.

But somehow, he was just unprepared for this.

He saw row after row of different animals in small cages. One large room was mainly a holding area where the animals were confined and prepped. It was difficult to see animals here that would normally be wild and running free, living their lives. The animals were scared and looked numb. Many were just staring into nothingness. But the real horror awaited them in the other rooms.

The laboratories.

While wiggling through one of the dark ducts, Ricky was startled to come across a single white mouse running towards him along the creased edges of the silvery metal.

"Oh, excuse me!" Ricky said after jumping in surprise, the ductwork making a loud metallic popping sound.

"Hello," the little mouse said in a hushed tone. "Keep quiet please."

"Sure, sorry," Ricky said apologetically. "Do you live here?" he asked as he adjusted the dim glow from his wristband to allow some more light.

"Not for long," the mouse replied. "I managed to get free from one of the humans a little while ago. She must have been new." He looked around in the dark beyond Ricky with large scared eyes to figure out a way to continue his escape. "Now if you'll excuse me, I'll be leaving this nightmare."

"Um, before you go," Ricky said quietly. "Can you help me to understand what is going on here?"

The mouse stopped in its tracks and looked mortified. "You *want* to know what's happening here? Some things cannot be unseen."

Ricky nodded in understanding. "I know, but I need to find out."

The mouse was staring back at him blankly.

"If you show me around a bit, I can show you the way I came in from the outside and you will be free," Ricky said, hoping the mouse would value a guaranteed path out.

"Ok, but let's do this quickly," the mouse said. "I've spent too much of my life in here already."

"Ok," Ricky replied. "Thank you."

"Follow me," the mouse said quickly, turning around in a flash and heading back the way it had come. "We'll start with where I came from."

Ricky followed, envying the small size of the mouse in such a tight space. His own raccoon fur was scraping the sides of the ducts wherever he went, collecting large lines of dust that accumulated and then fell off like dirty snowballs.

"I should send them a bill for cleaning their ducts!" Ricky said with the hopes of lightening the mood a little.

The mouse paused to look back momentarily. He was not amused. "Keep moving."

Finally, they arrived at one of the laboratory rooms and the mouse pointed through the vent for Ricky to look through. He saw numerous small cages filled with mice and rats.

"This is where they inject us with cancerous cells," the mouse said despondently. "See for yourself what that does to us."

Ricky looked at the various cages and their inhabitants. Many of the rats had grown huge tumors as a result. Some of them had large masses hanging off of their sides that almost doubled the size of the rat. Others had growths on their bellies that made it almost impossible to walk and hard to breathe. Some had hugely swollen necks and faces.

"How can they even eat?" Ricky asked with sadness in his voice.

"The humans use large plastic syringes to force-feed them every day," the mouse answered.

Ricky noticed that a few rats had taken to chewing off their tumors, which left them with huge open sores that oozed pus and blood. It was revolting.

"Ok, I'm getting the picture. Let's move on," Ricky said. He found it was hard to pull his attention away, but there was more to see.

"Here is the rabbit lab," the mouse said. "I've heard they test mostly chemical reactions on them since rabbits have very sensitive skin and eyes."

Ricky looked through the vent and saw some slightly larger cages with mostly small, white bunnies. There were a few others of all sizes and colors in the mix. In one area there were white rabbits that had large patches of fur shaved off. They must have been applying different chemicals to their skin to see what the reaction was. Many of them had bright red and inflamed areas on their skin.

The mouse put its tiny paws up on the vent and joined

Ricky in taking in the scene. "It looks like those poor guys can't even move," he said as he pointed to some rabbits that were held with metal restraints.

Ricky saw one of the human workers in a white lab coat shaking up a small eye dropper and move towards one bunny. Its eyes were held open while orange chemicals were dropped in from a purple gloved hand. Ricky saw their bodies tense with pain and shake in fear. It was unreal.

Ricky pulled his own paw back slowly from the vent. "This is horrible," he said.

"I know," the mouse replied. "There's more," he said as he scampered down another duct. Ricky followed with a growing sense of dread.

"The cats are in this one," the mouse said as they came up to another vent. They both looked through the slats and took in the scene below. For some reason there were cats that had their eyes or ears intentionally damaged and researchers were noting their reactions to various sounds. Their meows and screams were haunting.

Ricky had started to feel a bit of animosity towards cats in general with Minka's late night sessions, but this room brought his compassion flooding back. How could anyone torture innocent kittens like this? It was unconscionable.

"There is another one for dogs. They use them for testing chemicals and poisons," the mouse said grimly. "I'd really like to get out of here as soon as possible though."

"Ok, let's skip that one," Ricky said as he could hear them whimpering nearby. The mouse wasted no time and darted off in a new side duct.

"This way to the swine lab," the mouse said. "It's towards the back of the building."

After one of the longer ducts, they arrived and again peered through the vents. There were some small pigs that were kept in larger cages packed with straw as bedding. The smell was nauseating.

Ricky could only surmise that the scientists were conducting burn tests on their skin, as there were large metal canisters with colorful warning labels all around. The pigs had black grids marked on their sides, with charred areas of skin in each square. None of them were moving and Ricky couldn't tell if they were sleeping or dead.

"Ok, let's keep moving," Ricky said. He didn't want to stay any longer than he had to.

"The last lab is this way," the mouse said as it ran off down a side branch of the labyrinth. "To the primates."

Ricky followed, glad to be almost done with this house of horrors.

Through the vent they saw monkeys of various types in cages. For a brief moment Ricky thought that maybe the humans would have mercy on their closest relatives, but sadly that was not the case. Some were rocking back and forth or pacing around their cages in obvious distress. The lush green forests they would normally call home were replaced with steel cages. They had no semblance of a normal life.

Ricky heard a soft squeak from the mouse and glanced over at him. "You ok?" he asked with concern.

The mouse pointed towards one part of the lab. There were monkeys that had electrodes *implanted* into their brains. There were bundles of colorful wires that fed into nearby computers that displayed vivid patterns on the screens.

Ricky's utter shock was interrupted as the door to the lab opened and Dr. Katie Nova walked in with a bearded lab technician.

"Be very still!" the mouse said quietly but with urgency. "She's the one that runs this place."

"Dr. Nova?" Ricky asked, though he knew the answer.

"Yes," the mouse replied in a barely audible whisper. "She is the director of the entire facility, overseeing all of the different experiments."

Dr. Nova looked through the bars at the monkey with the electrodes and wires attached. "Have you administered the latest series of compounds?" she asked of the technician.

"Yes ma'am," he said as he nodded affirmatively. "We pumped it into their stomachs this morning."

She was now looking at the computer screens. "Good. Go ahead and start the aversive stimuli phase. Let's see how that affects their pain responses. Then put all the primates back in the holding area at the end of the day."

"Yes, ma'am," he repeated and started typing on the keyboard in front of the computer.

Abruptly the hands of the monkeys shook as they gripped the bars of their cages tightly. They looked utterly helpless.

Ricky gasped and backed away from the vent. He found himself thinking that a quick death from a hunter or butcher might be preferable to this living hell.

The mouse looked numb.

"Are you sure that this is Dr. Katie Nova?" Ricky asked.

"Yes, of course," he said quietly. "She goes in and out of every room and is involved with every facet of the day-to-day operations here. Others come and go, but she is the center of it all."

Ricky double-checked the name and the coordinates carefully on his wristband this time:

DR. K. NOVA
41.385N, -73.023W
6.01.2019
22:13 HRS
METHOD: INTERVENE

A sub-menu on the wristband gave him a detailed map of the building, and the exact location of intervention was in her glass office next to the animal holding area.

"She doesn't have a pet named Kiko Nova or something ridiculous like that, does she?" Ricky asked.

The mouse had a blank expression.

"Never mind," Ricky said.

There was no question - she was the target.

"Ok, follow me and let's get out of here," he said, slowly turning himself around and leading the mouse back out towards the air vent that he had come through.

They came to the large exterior vent and stopped just before it.

"Thank you for your help," Ricky said to the mouse as he pointed to the light filtering in. "This is the way out."

The mouse jumped up the vent and stopped for a moment to look back. "I'd recommend leaving this place right now and never coming back." With that, he squeezed through one of the slats and disappeared.

Ricky looked through the vent to see where the mouse had gone, but he was nowhere to be seen. He gazed further out to locate Emma. She was waiting with her bike just on the other side of a fence that was topped with wicked looking razor wire. They evidently didn't want anything to get in or out of this place.

Before crawling out of the vent, he sat in the duct for a few minutes. There was a steady stream of air being pulled in from outside, but somehow the air still smelled of the lab. Chemicals and sterilizer. Wood chips and excrement.

All of this was too much to take in. Ricky felt ill. More than that, he felt betrayed. Jake was right – this mission really was a farce. He should be here saving the poor souls in this lab, not the human whose job it was to torture them. He couldn't be complicit in this anymore.

After taking a moment to regain his composure, he opened the air vent and shimmied down the drainpipe to the ground. He then shook off the remaining dust from the ducts and briefly watched it float away in the breeze as a small cloud. He then moved as quickly as he could across the grass towards the fence and slid under the chain links where he had dug out a small trench earlier.

Emma was sitting on the ground next to her bike, playing with a yellow flower.

"How'd it go? Any better than the other two?" she asked optimistically.

"I'm afraid not," he said. "Let's head back to the shed and I'll give you the details."

"Ok," Emma said, placing the flower down gently. She could tell from Ricky's demeanor that things were not good.

She lifted him up into the bike's basket and they made the long ride home. Even on the bike it took a good half an hour. Ricky was grateful for the ride since there was no way he could walk this far in his current condition.

Back at the shed, Emma sat down with Ricky on the floor. He curled up into a furry ball with his paws wrapped around his legs and striped tail. Monique's bed was still empty.

"I can't do it," Ricky said softly. "I just can't."

"Was she that bad, this Dr. Nova person?" Emma asked sympathetically.

There was no point in withholding anything, so Ricky told her. He gave her every detail of the horrid lab and the tortures that were going on there.

Emma didn't know what to say. "Maybe we can call someone to make them stop?"

Ricky was shaking his head slowly. "No, evidently this is all legal in your society and goes on all the time in the name of science. I can't believe they are allowed to do this, but they are."

Emma straightened the blanket in Monique's empty bed thoughtfully as they talked. "Science should be for the betterment of the world."

"I agree!" Ricky said with a sigh. "I'm living proof that science can do amazing things. But why are so many humans convinced that this is ok to do to animals?"

"I don't know," Emma said. "Science is neutral, so can be

used for both good and bad. I think a lot of people see it as for the 'greater good', so it just goes on unchallenged."

"The greater good?!" Ricky asked with incredulity in his voice. "Maybe if these animals had a choice and volunteered for this. Maybe if there were absolutely no other way."

He took a moment to look out of the window, his eyes squinting in the light. "But they didn't volunteer – they were trapped or bred in captivity for the sole purpose of being mechanisms for human research. Some of these animals have never even stepped foot on natural ground!"

He turned back to Emma and looked at Monique's bed before turning away again. "And there are plenty of other methods to conduct scientific research. If you humans would just focus your attention on pursuing those you wouldn't have any need for this barbaric practice anymore!"

"I *know*, I agree. We need to make some changes," Emma said, getting somewhat defensive.

"Some?! It seems like your entire society revolves around the abuse and exploitation of helpless animals!"

"What do you mean?"

"You eat them when you don't need to, you kill them for fun, and you wear parts of their murdered bodies on yours because you think it looks good. You raise and torture them like they are objects with no value other than what they can do for humans!"

Ricky was shaking his head back and forth in his furry paws. "And to top it all off, it's destroying your world. Humans really are responsible for their own destruction."

Emma took a deep breath and tried her best not to get baited into another argument. "Does this mean you aren't going to save her?" she asked.

Ricky took a moment to compose himself. "I've decided. She's on her own. If she's slated to die naturally, then so be it," he said resolutely.

Ricky was holding out his furry paws as if counting on his fingers. "I saved the butcher, who has no doubt gone on to kill and dismember countless other innocent animals for profit. We saved the hunter… eventually the right one…who will now go on to hunt and kill more animals just for the fun of it. And if I save this woman, it is certain that she will continue to do the horrible things she is doing to those animals."

Ricky continued in a sullen manner. "Not only that, more and more will be bred for the sole purpose of these tortures. There is no end in sight, and I will not be a part of it. Jake was right – the mission is flawed. There must have been a mistake."

Emma didn't seem happy with his decision. "If you know that someone is about to be killed and you have the ability to save them, then you need to. Otherwise you are partly responsible for their death."

She gestured towards herself. "Just like me being responsible for the deaths of animals that went into the food I ate. I didn't do the killing myself, but my inaction and support of the system made it possible."

"I don't care," Ricky said firmly. "You didn't see what I saw. I don't think I can even go back to that place, let alone save the person who runs it."

Ricky's expression softened a little as he looked up at Emma. "Look, I know you are trying to help, and you have. You've done so much for me and for Monique that I can never repay."

He looked downward at his bandage and rubbed it with his paw. "But look at my leg. Look at what happened to Monique. We are literally risking our lives to accomplish this mission, but for what? What good has it done? What would happen if I got killed trying to save this woman? Is her life worth mine, or yours?"

Ricky took another deep breath and looked at the details on his wristband again. "Her appointment will come and go later tonight, and then tomorrow I will be recalled to my own time. I will accept whatever punishment they decide to bestow on me. But that's my choice. I am choosing this."

There was a moment of silence between them.

"So, there's nothing I can do or say to convince you otherwise?" Emma asked.

"No, I'm sorry, but my mind is made up," he replied.

"Ok," she said curtly. He knew he had disappointed her, but he just couldn't fathom continuing on with this.

Emma got up from the floor and dusted her pants off. "Get some rest and I'll see you tomorrow."

"Ok," Ricky said. He watched her turn around and exit the shed. Ricky realized she seemed older than she had just a few days ago. In all fairness, a lot had gone on in that short time.

Now there was nothing to do but wait.

CHAPTER NINETEEN: *THE TEAM*

Ricky was not sleeping well. Monique wasn't back yet, and his decision to not save the third target was still weighing heavily on his mind. His conversation with Emma hadn't gone very well either. She seemed so disheartened. He would have to make it up to her somehow before he left.

As he lay awake, he thought again about the second target, R. WOODMAN. Did Jake know that it was Rosco the dog all along? It was Jake who pointed him right towards Randall and got him off track. He supposed it didn't matter though. They did wind up saving him after all.

But poor Monique! He kept re-playing the scene in his mind. They were running in the field towards the woods. Monique turned to look back, and then fell as the shotgun blast hit her in the face. It was terrible to think about, but he couldn't help it. During the daytime he was able to get his mind off of the painful memory and focus on something else, but at night it was much more difficult. He passed in and out of consciousness and the memory always seemed to be there waiting for him.

He was almost glad for the distraction when his proximity alarm gave a squeeze on his wrist. Well, at least he could tell Minka that she was right all along. Would she gloat? Probably.

Only it wasn't Minka that came to visit. It was Rosco Woodman the dog.

He was poking his head through the flappy door at the edge of the shed and he seemed worked up about something.

"Um… hey coon. You in there? Hey. Wake up."

He tried to bump through the door but was too big to fit.

"Hey. Trash panda. Hey." He said in a low hushed tone.

He didn't look like he was a threat. "I'm here," Ricky said. "How did you know where to find me? What do you want?"

"Uh, I guess… well, the cat told me you were here. And I wanted to, um, say thank you. Um, for saving me." Rosco held his paw out and it was wrapped up professionally this time.

"You're welcome," Ricky said mostly as a courtesy. "You really didn't have to come in the middle of the night to tell me that though. Come back tomorrow and we can talk."

"Uh, that's not really why I'm here," Rosco said. "Well, it is, but that's not the uh, main reason."

Ricky was getting a little impatient, but it was obviously hard for this dog to be talking to someone who was up until recently a mortal enemy.

"Go on," Ricky said as calmly as he could.

"Master is a fireman, and he has this radio thing in the house that tells him when there is a fire. It makes beeping sounds and crackly sounds, and then it talks. I heard something about an explosion, and yeah, the fire nearby. Master went to work. To go help."

"Ok, that's great," Ricky said. "But why are you telling me this in the middle of the night?"

"Uh, because I think *your* master is there. The one with the bike that lives in that house. The radio said something about a bike and maybe a girl."

"Emma!!" Ricky cried out loud as he jumped up and threw the blanket off. "Oh, no!"

Ricky felt the panic rising in him. She must have decided to go to the lab on her own to save Dr. Nova!

"Oh crumbs, this is not good. I need to help her, but I have no way to get there with my leg like this," he said as he looked around the shed as if something in there could help.

"Sorry, but mine isn't any better," Rosco said, holding up his paw and examining it. He chewed on the bandage a little with his teeth.

Ricky needed help, desperately. Emma was in trouble, Monique was still at the animal hospital, and here in the shed they had two bum legs.

"Minka!" Ricky exclaimed. "Where did you see the cat?"

"Earlier I saw her on the porch of the house over there. She and that vermin squirrel like to hang out in there at night where I can't get to them."

"You need to lighten up on that squirrel," Ricky said seriously. "But never mind that now, I need to find them immediately."

Rosco backed out of the flappy door and Ricky came flying through it a moment later. They both hobbled across the yard towards the screened-in porch that was attached to the back of the house. The floor of the porch was a few feet off of the ground, and there was a small opening in the screen material that looked about cat sized.

Ricky leapt up as far as he could to the lip of the porch, and then hoisted himself up the rest of the way. The hole in the screen wasn't big enough for him, but he pushed through anyway. There was a faint zipper-like ripping sound as the hole expanded to raccoon size.

He took a few steps across the porch and noticed a soft light coming from underneath one of the patio tables next to where the grill was stored.

"So that's how Jake got to the grill to chew the hose! Focus, Ricky, focus," he said to himself.

As he got closer, the light got brighter, and he could see that not only was Minka there, but Jake as well! What on earth were they doing?

"Hey Ricky," Jake said casually.

"Hi trash panda," Minka said, leaning over sideways to get a better look at Ricky. "Should we deal you in?"

Ricky then saw that they had a small overturned bucket

between them, and they were playing some kind of card game. There was a pile of acorns and cat treats in the middle. Jake was sitting on a coffee can so that he could see over the top. He wasn't sure in the dim light, but Ricky thought Jake might be smoking a tiny cigarette.

"Emma's in trouble!" he managed to get out. "We need to find a way to get to her quickly!"

Jake seemed unfazed, but Minka was suddenly activated like a mama bear protecting her young. "What? Where?!" she shouted.

"The animal laboratory," Ricky said. "It took about thirty minutes on a bike, and I can barely walk more than a few minutes at a time. Rosco back there isn't any better."

Now it was Jake's turn to be activated. "Rosco the dog is here?! Now?" He leapt up from his seat and knocked the bucket over. Acorns and cat treats rolled everywhere.

"Yes, he's here, but I need you to put aside your differences right now. Emma is trying to save the third target, Dr. Nova."

"So, let her save her if she wants. I suppose that's her prerogative," Jake said uncaringly.

"You don't understand." Ricky said. "There was an explosion at the lab and it's on fire. Emma might be in trouble."

"Yes, we need to help her," Minka said determinedly. "I don't care about that Nova lady, but Emma means the world to me."

For once, finally, Ricky saw some compassion in Minka's face. Her eyes were wide, and she seemed genuinely concerned.

"Well, good luck with that," Jake said somewhat callously as he folded his arms. "I'm not going."

Minka turned to face Jake. "Do this and I'll give you access to the kitchen cupboards every night."

"Hmm… that's tempting and all, but…"

"*Do it* squirrel or I'm calling in all of your gambling debts," Minka said menacingly.

"I'm in," Jake said quickly.

"Great," Ricky said. "But how? How can we possibly get there in time to make any difference?"

"Let's travel the same way the humans travel," Minka replied. "Let's take the car."

"Ha! The car? Are you serious?" Jake asked with a laugh. "How in the world could we do that?"

"What do you say trash panda, can you use that fancy thing on your wrist to interface with her dad's car?" Minka asked.

Jake looked confused. "How can you possibly use a wristband to start and drive a car from this time?"

Ricky knew. "It's an electric car! Emma said so. That means that all of the controls are electronic. The steering, the brakes, the accelerator… everything! It might work!" he exclaimed gleefully.

"Then what are we waiting for?" Minka asked. "Let's do this thing!"

CHAPTER TWENTY: *A NIGHT RIDE*

*U*nder cover of darkness, the motley group of animals ran together around the house and gathered at the side of the sleek gray car in the driveway. Luckily it was parked outside tonight instead of in the garage. One less hurdle to jump.

Ricky looked over the assembled team and made mental notes of their different abilities. One raccoon, a dog, a cat, and a squirrel. It would have to do. He took charge and addressed the makeshift rescue team. "Every one of us will need to work together for this to work. Emma's life may depend on it."

"Minka," he said, turning to look at her.

"Yes, sir," she replied, sitting up straight. Wow! Her personality really flipped.

"What do we need to get into this car and make it go? Is there a metal key or something?" he asked.

"It's a Tesla," she replied with a hint of smugness. "It has a small key card that gives you full access. Emma's dad keeps it in his wallet."

Ricky thought about that for a moment. "Ok, Minka, you are the stealthiest cat I've ever met. I need you to go into Emma's dad's room and get that card. But you need to do it really quickly, and not wake him up."

"I'm on it," she said, disappearing into the night.

Rosco didn't look confident that this would work. "Um, can she really sneak up on a human who is sleeping and not wake them up? Anytime I try to do that with Master, it doesn't work.

My collar makes noise, my nails click on the floor, or he hears my panting."

Ricky let out a little laugh. "Oh yes, sneaking up on someone while they are sleeping is like her superpower."

Jake nodded his head in agreement. "Her nickname is *Kitty Soft Paws* around the neighborhood."

A few moments later, Minka was back, with a small black and silver card in her mouth. She dropped it into Ricky's outstretched paw. "Here it is."

"Wow, that was quick," Rosco said with respect in his voice.

"Told ya," Jake said.

Ricky smiled. "Nice work!"

Minka pointed up at the glass panel between the front and rear doors. "You need to hold it up to the pillar there, and the car will unlock."

"Ok," Ricky said. "Rosco, I need a bit more height."

Rosco took a few steps towards the car and let Ricky climb up onto his back. Ricky held the card up to the pillar, and almost instantly they saw the interior lights come on and the mirrors on the side of the car unfolded. The headlights at the front of the car beamed a brilliant white light into the trees across the street.

"We're in!" Ricky exclaimed in a hushed voice.

Ricky then pushed on the smooth silver handle in the door, and the door popped open. One by one, the entire crew piled into the car's white interior that looked spotless and smelled of new technology. Ricky sat in the driver's seat, Minka took the front passenger seat, and Rosco sat in the back behind Minka. Jake took a standing position on the center console between the two front seats.

Now that the car was unlocked, Ricky was able to interface with it through his wristband. He tapped furiously on the small screen at his wrist, as well as on the large touchscreen in the car. After a few moments his wristband displayed some blue letters: CONTROL INTERFACE ESTABLISHED. The main touchscreen of the car mirrored the controls so that the others could see it as well. The large map showed their current location and a bright blue path to the lab.

"Yes!" Ricky said with optimism, his furry face being lit by the glow of the large touchscreen.

Ricky raised up his seat as high as it would go and stood up to get a clear view over the dash. He was able to lean on the steering wheel and still work the controls on his wristband.

"Ok, here we go," he said while tapping his wristband again. On one side of the screen there was a vertical bar that controlled acceleration from zero to one hundred percent. He gently eased it up to three percent and the car silently rolled forward.

Rosco looked confused about what was happening. "I think, um, that you stalled it. It's supposed to make lots of noise and go fast."

"It's electric," Minka said dismissively in Rosco's direction. "So it doesn't kill the planet and sound like your annoying mud truck." Rosco looked down and away sheepishly. Jake snickered.

Ricky eased the car to the end of the driveway and initiated the turn into the street by rotating the outer disc of his wristband. He was leaning on the steering wheel and wasn't quite prepared for it to rotate under him.

"Whoops!" he said as his paws slipped off of the wheel and he had to catch himself before falling into the footwell.

"I guess I'll have to lean back against the seat here," he said as he continued to operate the controls gingerly and readjust his position. A moment or two later the turn was completed, and they started down the long straight road. It was deserted and mostly dark.

"Uh, trash panda, we really need to pick up the pace here," Minka said.

"Yeah," Jake said. "I can run faster than this. Like, I'm not even kidding."

Ricky took a moment to look around at the others, his whiskers twitching slightly. "Give me a break here, I've never driven a car before!" They all peered back with expectant looks to get things moving.

"Ok, ok, I'll take it up to five percent…" Ricky said as he started to slide the acceleration bar up slightly.

Jake exhaled impatiently and reached for the car's large touchscreen in front of him. "Just crank it up to one hundred and let's get this show on the… AAAAAAHHHHH!!!!!!"

His squirrel scream was followed closely by a thump as he flew through the air and impacted into the soft white cushion of the back seat.

The Tesla had violently launched to warp speed, sending all of the occupants flying backwards and flattening them against their seats.

"Oh my God!" Minka cried out.

"AAAACK!" was all that Ricky could manage to say.

"AROOOO!!!" roared Rosco as he used his paw to hit the window control so he could stick his head out of it.

Trees and lights passed by at a blinding pace as the unrelenting acceleration kept them all pinned. Ricky did his best to keep the car on the road, but it started getting closer and closer to the trees and poles that lined the street on the sides. Warning chimes were starting to sound as the car's sensors detected that dangerous obstacles were getting closer.

Jake finally managed to breathe again and let out a couple of chattering squirrel chirps. "Ok, maybe we can dial it down a little now!"

Ricky composed himself enough to peel his eyes off of the road for a moment and drop the acceleration control back down to ten percent.

With the sudden deceleration, Minka and Ricky breathed a sigh of relief, Rosco gave a grunt of disappointment, and Jake slid down into the back seat of the car next to him.

Minka could see that this wasn't going to end well. She gestured to Ricky and a lever next to the steering wheel. "Just push that black lever down twice to put the car in auto-pilot mode. It will drive itself and get us there. Alive."

"Good idea," Jake said.

"You tell me this now?!" Ricky asked incredulously. He double pressed the stalk and they heard a pleasant chime sound. The steering wheel icon on the touchscreen turned blue, and the car gradually sped up to a reasonable speed. It also turned the wheel left and right to follow the curves of the road.

They breathed a collective sigh of relief.

"Oh yeah. Much better," Jake said. "No offense, Ricky," he added.

"None taken. Let's just get there and help Emma."

With the car taking over control, it gave them all a moment to relax a little. There was nothing they could do until they arrived.

For Ricky it was somewhat surreal being here in this human's car, traveling through all of these trees with these odd companions. The sweet air from Rosco's window blew across his fur and he heard crickets and katydids singing in the night. It's too bad they couldn't have done this without the threat of danger to Emma.

It never should have come to this, he thought to himself. He would never forgive himself if she were hurt or killed. This was his mission. His responsibility. And he blew it. He let his emotions get in the way.

He needed to make it right.

CHAPTER TWENTY-ONE: *TRAPPED*

*T*he explosion was sudden and violent. Dr. Katie Nova had stayed late and had lost track of time. The lab typically got pretty quiet at night, with the stillness only punctuated by the occasional sound of small animals scurrying around through wood chips.

From her office in the holding area, she could hear even the slightest sounds as if they were mere inches from her ears. Laps of tiny mouse tongues at water bottles with small metal balls in the spouts. Soft whimpers from the dogs. The occasional tap-tap sound of a monkey swaying back and forth. These were all normal sounds that she had learned to tune out over the years.

Maybe the utter quiet made it worse, but nothing could have prepared her for the deafening blast that struck her seemingly out of the blue. There was a powerful shock wave as well that cracked the glass windows of her office and physically blew her backwards out of her chair. Papers and bits of acoustic ceiling tiles went flying everywhere.

Instantly her computer and every light went out all at once. The normally bright lab was plunged into darkness, only punctuated with blasts of light from flashing strobe units. Dim emergency lights came on and her eyes struggled to adjust. Soon after there was a wash of thick acrid smoke that filled the air.

Her ears were ringing from the blast, but as her hearing returned, she could pick out the piercing wail of the fire alarms.

Ear-splitting buzzes, beeps, and sirens that were tailor made to convey a sense of urgency.

"GET OUT!" they screamed in a universal language. Everything about the situation and in her DNA told her to run.

She struggled to get to her feet on trembling and weakened legs, bracing herself on her desk and slipping on the papers on the floor. As she got close to the door of her office, she saw across the lab the orange and red flames filling the main corridor.

It was blocked.

The smoke was getting thicker, but it was the sounds of the animals that made her choke and struggle to catch her breath. It was a cacophony of shrieks, squeals, and what sounded like screams. She saw frightened animals flinging themselves at the metal bars of their cages and running into glass walls trying desperately to find a way out. Her own shaking hand pressed on the shattered glass of her office enclosure as she took in the scene and panic set in.

They were all trapped.

A room full of frightened animals faced their impending doom.

One of them was named Katie Nova.

CHAPTER TWENTY-TWO: *THE LAB*

By the time Ricky and the rest of the rescue crew had arrived at the laboratory, a large part of the building was already engulfed in flames. There were red fire trucks with flashing lights and a handful of firefighters training water cannons on the building. Ricky took over control of the car and pulled it around towards the opposite side of the large building so that they wouldn't be seen.

A few drops of water appeared on the car's windshield and the automatic wipers came on to brush them away. Was that spray from the hoses or was it starting to rain?

"I think the fire is where the pig laboratory and the storage room are. There is also a loading dock there," Ricky said as they all exited the car to assess the situation.

Minka and Rosco went right up to the perimeter fence to get a better look. There was a popping sound like fireworks and a steady roar coming from the area of the fire.

Jake looked down at a detailed plan diagram on his own wristband. "Yup, that would make sense with all of those hazardous materials they store in there."

Minka looked back from her spot at the fence. "Where would Emma be?"

"I don't know," Ricky replied. "She could be anywhere in there."

"Maybe she never even went in," Jake said.

"There's only one way to find out," Ricky said, peering down at his wristband and then Jake's. "Our wristbands can pick up life signs, but there is a limited range. One of us will need to get closer."

Minka and Rosco looked up at the imposing razor wire that topped the tall fence in front of them.

"How did you get in before?" Minka asked as she pushed her paw against the metal chain link lattice.

"I dug a trench under the fence and slid under," Ricky said. "But that's on the other side of the building near where the humans are. We will need to dig a new hole. Rosco, can you do that?"

"You betcha, Boss. It will take some time with only one paw though."

"Ok, well get started," Ricky replied. "Make it big enough for a human to get through."

"Roger," Rosco said while nosing around the ground to pick a good spot on which to begin.

"Huh? No, *Emma*," Ricky said with confusion. "It doesn't matter – just dig."

Minka stifled a laugh and then looked at the fence and razor wire with an expression of concern growing. "That digging is going to take a few minutes and we don't even know if Emma is in there. We need to find her now."

"Leave that to me," Jake said confidently. "Getting into human buildings is *my* superpower."

Without a further word, he leapt up onto the fence and proceeded to run straight up towards the top. He then ran at full speed across the top of the fence, balanced on the chain links just below the coiled razor wire.

Jake then leapt to a nearby pole on the inside of the fence perimeter and spiraled his way higher and higher. Near the top there was a thin black wire that stretched from the pole all the way to the laboratory building, and Jake ran across it as easily as if it were a foot wide. After a few moments he disappeared out of view onto the rooftop of the building.

"I'm here," Jake's voice said from Ricky's wristband, startling both Ricky and Minka. "I'm getting over *three hundred* life signs in here, with two of them being human."

"One of those must be Emma," Ricky said. "The rest must be those poor animals in cages."

Minka nodded her head in agreement. "Let's get her out. Jake, where are the two humans located?"

"That might be an issue – they are in different rooms, and I can't tell which one is which."

"Well, we've got to start somewhere," Ricky said.

"Ok, sending the coordinates to you," Jake replied.

Ricky saw the locations on the map - one human was in Dr. Nova's office, and the other was in one of the laboratories. "Let's focus on the signal coming from the laboratory. That one is most likely to be Emma. Jake, head over there as quickly as possible and get a visual. I'll be there as soon as I can."

"I'm on it," Jake said.

"How's that hole coming, Rosco?" Ricky asked.

"Definitely big enough for you right now. I'll keep working on it though."

"Ok, I have my wristband and already know this building a little, so I'm going in," Ricky said. "Minka, you stay here with Rosco and keep a lookout for Emma and any other humans that might get in our way. Once we get her out, we might need your help to find this exact spot quickly."

"Got it," she replied.

Rosco paused his digging long enough for Ricky to slide under the fence. Once on the other side, he tried to run as quickly as he could across the expanse of grass between the fence and the building. His injured leg burned with the effort, but every second mattered.

As he ran, Ricky felt a few drops of water hitting his fur, and it became apparent that it wasn't from the firefighter's water hoses. Soon the grass was dancing and shimmering around him as drops of water pelted the ground with increasing frequency and intensity.

A moment later, a bright flash illuminated the whole of the

building for a split second. Almost immediately afterwards there was a crack of thunder so loud it made him duck and cringe as he ran. "Oh crumbs," he said to himself between heavy breaths. "That's the last thing we need."

Ricky found the downspout that led to the ventilation duct and started to climb. The rain made the smooth aluminum slippery, but his dexterous paws gripped tight. Even with an injured leg, there isn't anything that a determined raccoon can't climb!

The roar of the fire was getting louder and louder as he got higher up. Wisps of noxious black smoke blew by occasionally and Ricky had to hold his breath. There must have been some plastics and chemicals burning.

Ricky made it to the duct and started to crawl towards the lab. He checked his wristband frequently to make sure he was on track and to see where the fire was. The display was showing red and orange covering the entire area of the swine lab, the storage area, and the loading dock. The human he hoped was Emma was on the other side of the building, somewhat away from the fire. It was moving around as if trying to find a way out. A pulsing blue dot representing Jake had just made it to the edge of that room.

"Come in, Ricky," he heard Jake's voice say coming from his wristband.

"I'm here, Jake. I'm just a few turns away from you and the signal. Do you see her?"

"Yup, it's Emma," Jake said. "I'm looking out of a vent near the ceiling and see her on the far side of the room. There aren't any animals in this lab, just supplies and equipment. It looks like there are two doors, and she's beating the crap out of one of them with a swivel chair. It must be locked. I don't see any flames, but the room is definitely filling with smoke."

"See if you can call out to her and get her attention," Ricky said.

"I've already tried – with those alarms going off she can't hear me," Jake replied. Ricky could hear the piercing alarm sounds every time that Jake was talking. There were also some banging sounds that must have been Emma attacking the door.

Jake's voice came through again after a pause. "And I can't get the vent open. It's metal, so it would take me too long to chew through. I think you're going to have to bust through this."

"Ok," Ricky said. "I'm almost there. Go ahead on to the other signal and see if you can help Dr. Nova."

There was no reply from Jake for a moment. "You sure you want to help that woman? You've seen what she's doing here," he finally said.

"I know," Ricky replied. "But Emma was right. We are in a position to help, so we should. It's as simple as that. Let's finish the mission."

There was another pause from Jake. "Ok. I'm on it."

"Thank you, Jake," Ricky said. He saw Jake's blue dot head away from the lab and towards Dr. Nova's office via a smaller side duct.

A moment later, Ricky turned one last corner in the ductwork and saw a faint bit of light coming from a metal vent. The steady glow was punctuated with flashes of strobe lights. The smell of smoke was intensifying with every breath, and with every step the sirens got louder.

Finally at the vent, Ricky saw Emma across the room.

"Emma! Emma, over here!" he shouted. It was no use – she couldn't hear him over the sirens and the growing roar of the fire.

Ricky understood why Jake wouldn't be able to get through the vent. It was relatively thin, but it was still a substantial metal grill held in place by four large screws that were threaded through the folded duct's sheet metal in the corners. He slipped his paws in between the horizontal bars and tried to bend them apart. They barely budged. Jake was right – this called for some brute force.

Ricky braced himself against the vent and pushed against the other side of the duct. The sheet metal flexed a bit a first, and then refused to budge any further. He pulled back and then pushed all at once. He felt the impact through his entire body, but the vent started to move away from the duct slightly as the long screws slipped their threads.

Ricky pulled back, coiled up like a spring, and released again to maximize his impact. He hit with a bang. More movement! The top screws were mostly out, and the lower ones were starting to budge too.

"One more ought to do it," he said determinedly. "This one's for Emma."

Ricky coiled back again; arms outstretched to the sides. He aligned his good leg against the backside of the duct and put his bad leg in the corner. All at once, he pushed with all of his might on both of his legs and his paws.

"AAAAHHH!!" he yelled almost involuntarily as he flew towards the vent one final time. There was a momentary resistance from the vent that gave way as he went crashing through. The vent grill and Ricky started to sail through the air as their combined momentum carried them on a trajectory towards a workbench with some glass beakers and test tubes on it.

Ricky windmilled his paws backwards and tried to catch himself but wound up sliding and rolling across the tabletop and impacting a ridiculous number of glass containers on the way across. A split second later he disappeared from the bench and hit the floor with a crash.

After a moment, Ricky popped his head up and shook his fur to release some of the glass bits.

"Ricky!" Emma exclaimed gleefully, running across the room and scooping up the glittering raccoon and squeezing him in a joyous hug.

"Are you ok? You look like a fuzzy Christmas ornament."

"Yes, I'm fine. I think I just invented raccoon pinball," he said with a giggle. She laughed and hugged him even more. He hugged her back. It was so good to be with her again.

Reality then kicked in for Ricky "Are *you* ok? What were

you thinking coming out here on your own?! You could have been killed!"

"I'm ok. I know, but you had given me the information about her time of death, and I just had to do something," she said innocently. It was hard to argue with such purity.

"I know. But it wasn't your responsibility. It was mine," Ricky said with regret in his voice.

"Well, you're here now," she said with a grin. "Besides, I thought maybe she would fall down or choke on a hotdog or something, I had no idea the flippin' building would explode!" she said with a laugh that turned into a cough. It was getting more difficult to breathe.

"Yeah, let's get out of here," Ricky said, looking around the room. "You won't fit in the duct."

"I came in from the loading dock at that door." She said pointing to a door on the right about fifteen feet away. "But the door handle is too hot to touch now. The fire is burning in that back hallway. I soaked a lab coat in water and rolled it up to block the smoke at the bottom gap."

"Clever girl!" Ricky said proudly. Emma gave a little bow with mock humbleness.

"I don't know where this other door goes, but the handle is cooler. The problem is that it's locked," she said as she pointed towards the battered door on the left.

Ricky checked the map on his wristband. "That goes to the main hallway. That's our way out." Ricky ran over to the left door and noticed there was no keyhole or lock. There was, however, a small black plastic box with a tiny red light on it next to the frame of the door. "It's a proximity card lock. It works on an RF signal."

"Ok," Emma said. "But we don't have a prox card."

Ricky fiddled with his wristband a bit. "*I'm* your prox card – lift me up to that reader."

Emma put her arms around Ricky's sides and raised him up to the black box with the red light. Ricky held his wristband to the reader. A moment later, there was a beep from the box and the light changed to green. A clack of metal seemed to come from the door handle.

"It worked!" Emma exclaimed excitedly.

"Well, being from the future has its perks," Ricky replied nonchalantly.

Emma grabbed the handle and swung the door into the smoke-filled hallway.

They both looked at the map again and Ricky pointed to the main hallway that ran the length of the building. "The fire is to the right, so all we have to do is take a left up there and run straight out of the main entrance. Let's get you out of here."

"No," Emma said firmly.

Ricky looked puzzled. "What do you mean? If we try to go the other way, we will…"

"No, I mean I'm not leaving until I finish what I came here to do. We need to save Dr. Nova and all of these animals," she said resolutely.

"But the fire is spreading, and the humans can…"

"Ricky, no. They probably don't even know she is in here, and I don't think they would bother to save the animals."

That was a terrifying thought. "Those firefighters would leave them here to die?" he asked.

"I don't know," she replied. "Maybe, maybe not. All I know is that we are here right now, and we can do something about it. So let's do it."

Ricky looked at her with admiration. "Ok, Emma. Let's do this together."

"Together," she echoed.

"The rodent lab is right there beyond that door on the left," Ricky said while pointing. "Twenty feet ahead. Let's go."

Together they ran down the small hallway. They could feel the heat intensifying as they got closer to the source of the fire. Ricky went a few feet past the rodent lab door and took a quick look to the right. Further down the main hallway, bright flames mixed with black smoke as they billowed and licked at the walls and ceiling. Black water and debris were flowing on the floor and rapidly approaching down the hallway towards them. It must have been from the fire hoses or the building's sprinkler system. The smoke was thickest at the ceiling but was lowering towards them at a steady pace.

Back at the rodent lab door there was another prox card box. Without hesitation, Emma lifted Ricky up to the box and he held his wristband out. A beep, a green light, and the release of the lock followed.

Inside the lab, they could see the rows and rows of frightened rats and mice in metal and glass cages around the perimeter. In the middle were solid workbenches with hard black tops and various wooden drawers below. There was a collection of various electronic devices and glassware on the benches.

Ricky gestured to the highest rows of cages. "You start up there and I'll get the lower ones. As quick as you can!"

"Yup!" Emma replied. She then started to unlock the metal latches on every cage. Furry hooded rats and white mice poured out quickly, scaling down the metal bars and even leaping on her and crawling down.

"Their little rat feet tickle!" she said squirming and dancing as she continued to work the latches.

"Everyone!" Ricky said to all of the animals. "Go left out of this door and again left all the way down the long hallway. Wait for us at the main entrance and we will be there soon."

Obediently, the rodents poured out of the room like a river of fur. There were so many of them!

"Get the ones on the workbench way over there," Ricky said as he pointed to some rats that must have been in an active overnight study at the far end of the room. Emma ran over and popped the screened tops off of the glass enclosures and the rats quickly ran out with a few squeaks.

"They said *thank you*," Ricky said as he watched them run by towards the door.

Emma smiled and was suddenly reminded of Herbert, her dissected frog from her biology class. Now she was finally making a difference.

She then started to jog towards Ricky and the door.

"Ok, now on to the next area," Ricky said as he turned to leave.

That's when the second explosion happened.

It blew Ricky backwards and he tumbled into the cages next to him with a crash. A little dazed, he stumbled to his feet and looked around.

"Emma! Where are you?!" he cried out. She was just there a moment ago, and now she was gone.

Ricky ran around the workbenches in the middle of the room and saw her lying on the floor. He was there in an instant.

"Oh, Emma! Are you ok?" he asked frantically.

She didn't respond.

He noticed a gash on her temple and a bit of blood trickling down.

"Emma! Can you hear me?!" he asked in desperation as he put his ear to her chest and listened for signs of breathing. The sirens made hearing anything difficult, but he used his paw to block one ear while he listened with the other pressed tight against her. He heard both her heart beating strongly and steady breaths.

"Oh, thank goodness," he said. She was alive but unconscious. He patted her face a few times to see if he could rouse her, but she was out.

Ricky remembered his emergency medical training and rolled her to her side to ease her breathing. That would also prevent her from aspirating if she were to vomit.

He then quickly thought about his options. He needed to get her out of the building and quick. He tried to hold onto her arm and heaved to see if he could drag her out, but she was much too heavy for him. Her limp body barely moved.

"Jake! Come in," Ricky said into his wristband.

"Here," Jake replied.

"What's your status?" Ricky asked.

"I found Dr. Nova in her office, but the fire in the main hallway is trapping her. I've been trying to figure out how to get her out. Currently she's curled up in a ball on the floor. I think she's given up."

"I have a problem here too," Ricky said with distress in his voice. "I found Emma, but I think she hit her head with that explosion. She's alive, but now she's unconscious. She's too heavy for me to drag."

"It sounds like both of us have the same problem," Jake replied. "There is only so much we can do when they are so much bigger than us."

Ricky thought hard about their resources and options. Then a crazy plan occurred to him.

"Jake, I want you to go to the main entrance. You'll see a bunch of rats and mice waiting for one of us to unlock the door. Use your wristband to override the prox card interface that locks the door, then prop it open. Get them out and direct them to Minka and Rosco."

"Got it," Jake replied. "But what about the two humans and the rest of the animals?"

"Go with the rats and mice and let me know when you are out there at the fence. I'll work on releasing the rest of the animals in here in the meantime. I'll then give you further instructions."

"Ok, Jake out."

Ricky hated the thought of leaving Emma even for a second, but at the moment there was nothing that he could do for her, and he knew that she would want him to save the other animals.

He patted her on the cheek gently.

"We'll get you out. I promise."

CHAPTER TWENTY-THREE: *GRUDGES*

Outside, the rain had turned to a deluge. Torrents of rain fell and soaked everything and everyone. Somehow, between the rain and the water from the firefighter's hoses, the fire raged on seemingly unabated. Clouds of orange and black rose from the building and swirled in twisty columns. Puffs of flame and blasts of heat occasionally spurted from the building as compressed gas canisters exploded.

Sopping wet, Rosco and Minka stayed on task. Rosco kept having to dig at the trench under the fence to keep it clear of mud. It seemed like as soon as he got it clear, the sides would collapse in and he would have to start all over again. Occasional flashes of lightning and cracks of thunder made him jump and whimper, but he kept digging like somehow that would keep him safe.

Minka was keeping a close eye on the building, looking for any sign of movement. Her silky black and white fur was matted down close to her body, which made her body look frail and thin. But her eyes were strong with purpose. She would do anything for Emma.

During a pulsing flash of lightning, she thought she noticed something at the main entrance. Was that movement? It was so hard to tell with the rain pounding the grass and spraying up at the edges of the building. Another bolt of lightning and it was confirmed.

"I see something!" she yelled.

Rosco paused in his digging to take a look. A thunderclap shook the ground and made him cower. "I don't see anything... but your cat eyes are better than mine in the dark." He whimpered and continued to dig.

Minka knew she needed to signal them so that they could find the hole under the fence right away. She ran back to the open door of the car and perched on the wet driver's seat. She reached for the black lever next to the wheel and pulled it back and forth a bunch of times. The headlights of the car flashed bright light towards the entrance of the building, and she could see the blurry mass getting larger.

A few moments later she could see Jake at the front of the pack, leading the way. There were dozens and dozens of rats and mice following closely behind.

"Where is Emma?" Minka asked with concern. "Where is Ricky?"

Jake slid quickly under the fence and gestured for the column of rodents to do the same. They poured through and collected in a grassy area near the car. Some of them collapsed with the effort of running, while others raised their faces to the sky and held their paws out to feel the rain beat down on them.

For many, this was the first time they had ever left a cage. A small mouse held a green blade of fresh grass and seemed to be fascinated with how it bounced and swayed in her paw. A pair of older rats held each other and cried.

Jake turned from the refugees to face Minka. "Emma and Dr. Nova are trapped inside. Ricky is working on freeing the other animals. They should be coming out soon, so you will need to keep signaling them as they appear."

"What?! Is she ok?" Minka asked with alarm in her voice.

"I think so, but we need to get her out."

Jake then raised his wristband and signaled to Ricky. "I'm at the fence with Minka and Rosco. The first batch made it out safely."

Ricky's voice came through with the wail of sirens in the background. "Ok, good. Now I need you and Rosco to get the humans in here."

"Um… come again?" Jake said. Rosco stopped digging and looked up at Jake. He tilted his head with a confused dog expression that looked like he had mastered with years of dedicated practice.

Ricky knew what the problem was. "Look, this isn't the time for grudges. As much as I hate to do this, I need you and Rosco to go get Randall Woodman and get him to enter the building. That's the only way we can save Emma in time."

Jake squinted in the rain and stared at Rosco. The thought of working with both Rosco *and* Randall Woodman was staggeringly abhorrent.

Ricky continued. "Jake, I know you miss Isabelle. I know these two are responsible for her death. He shot and almost killed Monique, and she's *my* Isabelle. I can't change that, and neither can they. But Emma is my friend and she is going to die if we don't get Randall to help her."

Jake broke his staredown with Rosco for a moment and saw Minka walking up to him. She looked strangely helpless in a way he had never seen.

"Please do this," she pleaded on the verge of tears. "I know the humans are terrible sometimes, but I also know Emma. She came to this lab to save that woman *and* every animal in there. Look at all of them – we are here, and they are alive because of her."

Jake looked at the huddled furry masses and they peered back with grateful eyes.

Minka continued. "If *you* were trapped inside, she would do anything in her power to save you."

"Jake?" Ricky asked from the wristband.

"I'm here…" Jake said.

After a moment he finished. "Yeah, I'll do it."

Minka breathed an audible sigh of relief and sat down in the mud next to a large rat. Their eyes met briefly, and the rat cozied up next to her. He then extended his paw and patted her on the back. "There, there," he said reassuringly.

"Tell anyone and you're dead," Minka said.

"Of course," he replied.

Minka put her arm around him and shielded him from the rain.

"Ok, let's go mutt!" Jake yelled. Rosco perked his ears up and trotted over cautiously. Jake then leapt up on Rosco's back and grabbed his collar like a rodeo clown riding a bull.

Rosco looked back at the small squirrel on his back. "I'm not a mutt, I'm actually a pure…"

"I don't care! Mush!!" Jake smacked his wristband which emitted a small blue spark that zapped Rosco's flank and spurred him into motion.

"YIPE!" Rosco yelped out as he bolted towards the firefighters and their big trucks at a decidedly rapid pace.

CHAPTER TWENTY-FOUR: *KIM*

Ricky hoped that Jake would indeed go through with it and get the humans to help. In the meantime, he needed to save the rest of the animals.

Now that the front door was unlocked and propped open, he only needed to release the latches on the cages and tell them where to go. The rodent lab was cleared out, so next he went to the feline and canine labs. Without Emma's help it took longer to reach all of the top cages, but since the dogs and cats were larger in size, there were less cages with fewer animals to work through. Like clockwork, grateful animals dropped out of their prisons and ran to freedom in the stormy night.

The next lab had "LAGOMORPHS" on the door. Inside were the poor rabbits being subjected to terrible skin and eye testing. Again, Ricky worked through cage after cage, row after row, releasing the bunnies to safety. Some of those that couldn't see had to rely on others to lead them. A steady flow of furry animals passed through the hallways and out to Minka's guiding light by the fence.

Finally, there was one more room to clear – the animal holding area that led to Dr. Nova's office. The main door to the holding area was blocked by the ever-increasing flames, so Ricky had to get creative. He made his way back to the empty lab where he had broken through the vent and climbed back into the ductwork. From there he could access almost any room.

After a few minutes of crawling and coughing, he found another ceiling vent that opened out to the front of the holding area near the door. The heat was intense here and the smoke was chokingly thick.

He saw a variety of animal cages with frightened occupants all around, and there, on the floor of her glass office on the other side of the room, was Dr. Nova.

She appeared to be crying and shaking in a huddled ball. It instantly reminded Ricky of some of the animals he had just seen, trapped in their cages and helpless over their lives. He almost felt sorry for her.

Since he wouldn't be able to directly help her anyway, he thought it best to start with the animals nearest to him and the hallway door. Some were lying still, while others were still circling in fear or trying in vain to break out of their cages.

Fortunately, the vent in this room was slightly ajar and looked less secure than the first. He knew what it would take to get through, so he set right into pushing and slamming into it. After a couple of hits, the top screws had popped out and the vent swung down and away on one remaining screw at the bottom.

With a small leap, Ricky was able to land on top of the closest row of cages. He crawled to the front edge and peered over to see if there was an occupant. From his upside-down view he looked inside the cage and saw a small black and white monkey looking right back at him from the rear of the cage.

"What are you?" the monkey asked timidly.

"Uh, Ricky the raccoon here," he replied. He realized this poor monkey had probably never seen any animal other than the ones in cages at this facility.

"Raccoon? Never heard of it."

"How about… trash panda?" Ricky asked while arching his eyebrows.

The monkey scrunched its face a little. "Don't think so. Doesn't matter much anyway, we don't have long before we are all indistinguishable from each other."

This monkey was smart and had evidently accepted its fate.

"Maybe you can help me to get everyone out," Ricky said. "I'm from the outside and have a way to save us. What's your name?"

The small monkey got up from the back of the cage and made its way to the front, squinting from the heat of the nearby flames. "Name? I'm CM916. At least that's what they call me when the humans take me out."

Ricky looked at the tag on the front of the cage and saw CM916 FEMALE CAPUCHIN.

"Oh. How about I call you… Kim for now? It's a bit faster."

"Sure, I like that," Kim replied.

Ricky stretched a bit further and was able to slide the latch open to Kim's cage. The metal door swung open with a slight squeak.

"Ok, now go open up all of the latches on the upper cages," he said to Kim. "I'll get the lower ones." Ricky then climbed down to the floor and started to open every cage as eager faces looked on from every direction.

Kim reached her hands to the edges of her cage and looked all around at the room. Occasional flashes of orange flames burst past the door to the hallway, and thick smoke was rapidly filling the room.

She grabbed onto the bars of the neighboring cage and pulled herself close to the latch. From the inside of the cages they couldn't even see the latches due to a large plate that blocked that entire area from their reach. But on the outside, it was so easy – just a little upward motion and a slide to the side to open the latch. The door swung open readily and her neighbor CM915 was out.

Soon, Kim was making quick work of each latch and a growing collection of animals was pooling in the middle of the room on the floor. Dogs, cats, mice, rats, rabbits, and monkeys huddled together waiting for further instruction on how to get out.

Ricky knew that most of the animals could easily climb

back up to the vent and exit the way that he had come, but not all. There were some beagle puppies that had limited to no climbing abilities.

"This might be challenging," he said to himself.

CHAPTER TWENTY-FIVE: *FAILURE*

Jake and Rosco moved silently through the rain and got close enough to the firefighters to hear them talking to each other. They milled around the huge red trucks that idled with the steady purr of diesel engines.

"Dispatch, where is that hazmat unit?!" One of them yelled impatiently into the radio at his collar. Jake and Rosco couldn't hear the reply, but the firefighter didn't seem happy with whatever answer they had given.

"We're on the A-Side but can't go in until they get here and clear us to breach. There's a ton of accelerant in there and we need foam. There must be some Class B materials in there, and God knows what else."

Another firefighter was moving hoses around and making connections at the side of the big red truck. "Line charged!" he yelled after opening a big valve.

Jake steered Rosco around in their search for Randall. He saw Emma's bike propped up next to one of the smaller support vehicles in the back.

"Why aren't they going in?" Jake asked Rosco as they trotted around on the fringe of the woods to stay out of sight.

"They have all kinds of rules. They don't go in if it's too dangerous. They just let the fire burn itself out."

"Well, we need to change their minds," Jake said. "Let me know when you see Randall."

A few moments later Rosco gave a little woof and pointed

his nose towards a firefighter resting on the bumper of one of the trucks. "There he is!"

Jake started to feel a strange rhythmic vibration coming from his steed below. He turned around and saw that Rosco's tail had started to wag enthusiastically.

"Oh, brother," Jake said dismissively and jumped off of Rosco's back. "Go over there and do whatever it takes to get him to go inside the building."

"Roger," Rosco replied.

He then took off running towards Randall, barking the entire way. It got his attention almost immediately.

"What the... Rosco, is that you?" Randall said as he stood up and put his helmet down on the muddy ground. He started walking towards the dog and saw his unmistakable bandage.

"What the Hell are you doing out here?"

Rosco kept barking and gesturing towards the building with his nose. When that didn't work, he started running up towards the burning building and then back towards Randall.

"Come! Rosco, get over here! Come!" Randall yelled in vain as he walked closer to both the dog and the building. As soon as he got close, Rosco would bolt in a new direction.

"What are you doing? Come!"

Rosco knew exactly how to play this game and he was really great at it. Sometimes he would squeeze out of his collar and Master would chase him all over the woods for hours. Good times.

But now he was limited in where he could run. He needed to get Randall to go into the building. He sat facing the building and kept up a barrage of barking. He must get the hint from this.

Only he didn't.

Jake watched as Randall got closer to Rosco. In an impressive move given his full fire gear, he leapt and grabbed Rosco's collar, nearly tackling him to the wet ground.

"Gotcha! Now get back here," he said as he practically dragged Rosco back towards the truck. Rosco tried to bark a bit more as his paws slipped on the wet grass and mud, but he was starting to get the hint that it just wasn't working.

"Well that's just great," Jake said out loud to no one in particular.

CHAPTER TWENTY-SIX: *RESCUE*

Ricky had tied a series of white lab coats together and had hung them from the air vent cover that was still holding on by the lower screw. He then draped the coats over the front of the cages, making a makeshift rope that the animals could climb up. The monkeys went first and had instructions on how to get through the maze of ducts. The mice and rats climbed up the coats with no problem, and the cats followed shortly after.

Kim the monkey stayed with Ricky and the four beagle puppies on the floor. As the last kitten disappeared out of sight, Ricky turned to Kim.

"Ok, now for the hard part. We need to get these dogs out of here. They can't climb, so I will need to carry them. But they are too big for me to hold in my mouth while climbing."

"How about we use another lab coat?" Kim asked. "They have big pockets that we could put the puppies in, one at a time if needed, and you could wear it like a human would."

"Great idea! But we used all of them for the rope. We will have to take one of them off, which will take time since they are all twisted up now."

Kim looked towards Dr. Nova's office. "There is one more lab coat in there."

Ricky paused for a moment, hesitant to even go near Dr. Nova.

"I don't think that's such a good idea. I'll get started on…"

"It's ok. I'll go." Kim said, and started walking towards the office.

With the sirens still blaring, it was relatively easy for Kim to walk past Dr. Nova without her noticing. The human was curled up in a ball on the floor and was visibly shaking. Her breathing was ragged and punctuated with coughs and sobs.

Kim walked around the back of the desk and grabbed the spare white lab coat that Dr. Nova kept on a thin black coat rack. It fell to the floor in a soft pile that Kim scooped up and carried off towards Ricky.

"Here," she said once she returned to the holding area. They then worked together to get the lab coat onto Ricky. It was ridiculously long on him, but they tied up the sleeves and shortened it using the thin white belt from the waist.

They loaded up the first beagle in the oversized pocket, and Ricky began the climb. It was hard going with the extra bulk and weight but wearing the lab coat gave him the use of all of his limbs. Once at the top he helped the pup to get fully into the vent.

"Wait right there and I'll be back in a minute with your siblings," Ricky said to the puppy.

"Ok," the beagle replied with a tiny voice.

Ricky slid back down the coats to the floor and they loaded up the next dogs in the same manner. By the time they loaded up the last dog, Ricky's muscles ached, and his lungs burned with the choking smoke. But he made it to the top.

He suddenly thought of Emma and hoped that she was still ok. He wanted to get finished as quickly as possible so that he could go back to be with her.

"Ok Kim, that's the last of them. Come on up and let's go."

Kim was on the floor in the middle of the animal holding area, looking back towards Dr. Nova.

"What about her?" she asked.

Ricky turned towards Dr. Nova and then back to Kim. "We can come back and help her once we get these dogs out. Come on, we need to go."

Kim wasn't moving. She just kept looking back at Dr. Nova

on the floor a few feet away.

Ricky was suddenly reminded of his very similar argument with Emma about saving this human. Look what trouble that caused! He also remembered how he ultimately came to respect Emma's decision for compassion.

"She is frightened like we were. I will stay with her," Kim said determinedly.

Ricky was astounded. "After all that she has done to you and these other animals, you want to risk your life to comfort her?"

"Yes."

Ricky felt a swell of admiration for this tiny monkey. "Ok, well I've got to get these dogs out of here and down on the outside. I'll be back after that and we will see what we can do."

"I understand. Good luck," she said.

"Thank you for your help, Kim," Ricky said sincerely.

"You're welcome," she replied.

Ricky and the dogs disappeared into the depths of the vent while Kim started to walk slowly towards Dr. Nova. She was still shaking and obviously in serious distress. The foul-smelling smoke was everywhere now and inescapable. The sirens continued their wailing song.

Kim slowly stepped around the rubble of ceiling tiles and broken glass to get close. She then reached out and started to gently stroke and pet Dr. Nova's long black hair. She must have felt it and raised up her head suddenly with wide eyes and an expression of panic on her face as she tried to slide away on the hard, slippery floor.

Kim was startled and backed up a little, but then moved slowly and deliberately forward again with her arms outstretched.

"Hu… how… how did you get out of your cage?" Dr. Nova asked, not expecting an answer. "And… where are the other animals?" she asked incredulously as she peered around the doorway of her office and saw row after row of opened and empty cages.

Kim, being unable to answer in any way that Dr. Nova could understand, simply climbed up on her and put her small furry arms around her neck in a loving gesture.

It didn't answer her questions, but somehow that didn't matter.

CHAPTER TWENTY-SEVEN: *USELESS ANIMALS*

Jake watched as Rosco sat in the rain on the muddy ground next to the fire truck, looking utterly defeated and miserable. Randall had tied him up with a length of rope to the bumper and was getting his gear back on to take his shift on hose duty.

"Now stay there until I get back," Randall said sternly. Rosco looked up with sad eyes and cowered a little. It hurt to have upset Master.

As Randall walked away, Jake took the opportunity to run up to Rosco and hide from the rain under the protection of the truck's huge wheel arch.

"We need to kick it up a notch," Jake said.

"What do you mean?" Rosco asked hesitantly. "I don't want to disappoint Master any more than I have already."

"Believe me, dog, once we are finished here your Master is going to be proud as punch with you."

"Really?" Rosco asked with hope in his eyes.

"Definitely. But we need to act quickly."

Jake looked around from the cover of the wheel well and saw Randall working one of the large black water hoses at the side of the main fire. The other firefighter who was talking on the radio earlier was helping him.

"Let's see if this helps..." Jake said mischievously as his furry tail pulsed a few times. He tapped away on his wristband for a few moments, and then held it up to his mouth.

"Ah, Unit Two this is Dispatch. Come in Unit Two."

Jake saw the man with Randall lower the hose to respond to the radio at his collar.

Randall had turned off the hose nozzle to listen.

"Dispatch, Unit Two here, over," the man said.

Rosco's eyes went wide as he watched Jake continue the conversation.

"Yeah, Unit Two, we received a report of multiple occupants that will need extrication and rescue from the structure. Use forcible entry if required."

"Uh, Dispatch, what occupants?" the man said, looking to Randall with a confused look on his face. "It's an empty lab. We are still waiting on Hazmat here, entry has not been cleared, over."

Jake continued. "We've got a report of numerous animals in there that need immediate rescue. Also, possibly a young female."

"Uh, Dispatch, that's a negative on the female. Just an abandoned bike in the woods. Repeat we are waiting on Hazmat. Will breach when cleared for entry."

The man released the radio call button with a snap and looked over at Randall.

"Like we're going to risk our skin for a bunch of useless animals."

Randall blinked away the rain and looked back towards Rosco at the truck.

The man continued. "Heck, this is a barbecue! Don't you smell the bacon? Grab some beers and pull up a seat! Ha!"

Randall dropped the hose nozzle in the wet grass and walked away.

"Hey, where you going, Randy?" the man said with a baffled look.

Randall just kept walking.

CHAPTER TWENTY-EIGHT: **ALL THE DIFFERENCE**

*B*ack inside, Ricky was returning from delivering the dogs through the ductwork and saw Kim and Dr. Nova in the doorway of her office. He proceeded to the vent opening right in her office to get as close as possible.

Dr. Nova was sitting up now and holding onto Kim as if she were a precious human child that she hadn't seen in years. Tears rolled down her cheeks and left clear tracks on her skin as they washed away small channels of dirt and soot from the smoke. She was swaying gently back and forth as if trying to soothe both herself and the small monkey.

"Thanks to Kim she is coming back around. Now to get them out." Ricky said to himself. "Dr. Nova won't fit in the duct, and the only exit is blocked by fire. The walls are concrete block. What would Emma do? Think, think…"

Ricky tried to take a deep breath to clear his mind, but the increasing smoke made him cough.

"Wait, what *did* Emma do?" he asked himself as he thought back to that first lab with the fire on the other side of the door. Emma had rolled up a lab coat and soaked it with water to stop the fire and smoke at the bottom of the door. Why not do the same with Dr. Nova? She was conscious and could walk – she just needed protection from the flames and smoke for a few moments to get out into the main hallway.

Ricky tapped at his wristband a bit and set it to amplify his voice. He then backed up a little bit so that he wouldn't be visible if she happened to look up at the vent.

"Dr. Nova!" he called out. His voice was booming and loud in the enclosed duct.

No response.

He tried again. "Dr. Nova, can you hear me?"

Then he heard a soft reply muffled by the sirens. "Yes, I'm here. Who is that?" Her voice was getting louder as she moved closer to the vent. "Where are you?"

Ricky had to come up with something quick that she would believe.

"Uh, this is… Randall Woodman with the fire department." The thought of portraying Randall wasn't appealing, but he needed something. "I'm one room over and talking to you through the air duct. Can you walk?"

"Yes, but the doorway is blocked by the fire and the room is filling up with smoke. Please hurry," she said.

"Ok, we are going to get you out of there. I'm going to need you to follow my instructions quickly."

"Can't you just come in here to get me?" she asked. There was still marked fear in her voice.

"Unfortunately, no. We can't get in any further, so we need you to come out on your own. But I'll tell you exactly what to do and I'll be here to guide you."

"Uh, ok," she said worriedly. "What should I do?"

"First, I want you to look in the animal holding area for a large red cabinet that has a fire extinguisher in it. Try to stay low to the ground to minimize your smoke inhalation," he said.

Dr. Nova put Kim down and took a few steps out of the office to look around. She had to shield her face from the intense heat coming from the growing inferno in the hallway. Flames were starting to reach through the doorway and lick at the ceiling.

"Yes, it's by the hallway door. But I don't think that's going to be enough to put out the fire. And it's so hot in there I can barely get near it."

Ricky looked quickly at the map on his wristband. "Ok.

There is a small bathroom off of your office, yes?"

"Yes," she replied.

"I want you to go in there and take off your lab coat. Soak it in cold water and you can use it as a temporary shield against the heat."

"Ok. Wait…how did you know I'm wearing a lab coat?"

Oops! Ricky thought to himself.

"Uh, just a guess," he said, trying to sound casual. "Scientists always wear those things, right? Anyway, the cold water will help protect you. Do that as quick as you can. There is another vent in there, so we should still be able to talk."

"Ok," she replied.

Ricky gave her a few moments and then wriggled his way closer to the bathroom vent, still staying out of sight. He could hear the water running and some splashing sounds.

"Ok, it's good and soaked. Should I put it on?"

"Yes. Then splash as much water as you can on your face and your hair too. The more the better. Let me know when you are ready for the next step."

He gave her a few more moments to do this. Then waited some more.

"Dr. Nova are you ready?" he asked.

She didn't reply.

"Dr. Nova? Are you ok?"

Again, no reply. If she passed out from smoke inhalation his whole plan would be ruined.

Ricky wriggled further into the duct to risk a glance through the vent to see what was going on.

To his surprise, Dr. Nova was not unconscious, but was instead staring at herself in the mirror. The black soot was mostly cleared from her face but stained her lab coat in long gray trails. Her dark hair was sopping wet and was plastered to her face in dripping cords. Her blue eyes were piercing as they stared back at themselves.

"Dr. Nova?"

She sniffled a little and furrowed her brow in a despondent

expression. "I shouldn't be here."

"I know. That's why we are going to get you out. Next, we…"

"No, I mean *here*, in this lab. Doing this work with these animals," she said as she squinted slightly. "No, that's not accurate. Doing this *to* these animals."

"Uh, we don't really have time for this right now," Ricky said. "Let's get you out first and then…"

"I thought it was for the greater good," she continued.

"The greater good?" Ricky echoed.

"Yes, a small sacrifice for the benefit of many. Curing cancer, stopping Alzheimer's, lengthening life. That's why I chose this field and pursued this work. When did it become so fruitless? So cruel and pointless?" she asked.

Ricky didn't know what to say, so he just let her keep going.

"I haven't cured cancer," she said despairingly. "In fact, all I've done is give cancer to more animals than I can count. Sure, we've made some progress, but at what cost of life? How much suffering have we caused? Was there no other way to do it? Besides, more and more we are simply doing animal testing for cosmetics and drugs that even if successful won't be saving any lives."

Ricky was about to implore her to postpone this dialogue again, but something made him stop. She was finally realizing what she was actually doing here in this lab.

"Maybe I don't deserve to be saved. Maybe I should go down with the ship."

Ricky knew she was falling back into despair. He needed to get her back into a state of mind where she could function. "Of course you deserve to be saved, and I'm going to help you. Let's just…"

"I've ended so many lives I can't even begin to count how many," she said sadly. "I've caused unimaginable suffering to creatures that feel pain and fear just like us." She looked over at Kim in her office as she said this. "Do you *really* believe I deserve to be saved?"

Ricky had to pause for a moment. It was hard to face, but he had made the exact same decision himself. He had decided to let her die when he abandoned the mission.

He had made that decision to let her die for the greater good of the animals. A small sacrifice for the benefit of many. Just like her rationalizing that her work would save lives. The same logic was at play in both cases.

He then realized that in both cases it was just... *wrong*. Sacrifice for the benefit of others is truly noble, but it has to be a choice by the one making the sacrifice. If the animals in this lab had chosen to volunteer for these experiments, then yes, it could be worth it. But they had no choice. They never did.

If Dr. Nova chose to die to save the animals, then that too might be worth it. But she had the choice – it was hers to make. The questions rang in his mind. Does she really deserve to live? Should he just let her die?

Ricky was firm in his decision before. But now that he was here, looking at her, seeing her fear and suffering, it was different. That made it real. That made it personal.

It was like the difference between picking up a package of meat in the store – all wrapped and sterile with a nice branded label on it, versus seeing a living animal and killing it yourself to eat its flesh.

From a distance you can rationalize it. You can normalize it when you don't see what really happens. But up close it's different. It's different when you can look into their eyes and see the fear. See their body tense and shake. Seeing them facing their own mortality. It's different to watch someone die, knowing that you could save them. It's different when you can't just ignore the reality of what is really happening.

"Maybe you can change. Maybe you can now work *for* the animals," Ricky said.

She seemed to consider this for a brief moment.

"No, I don't think I can ever overcome how much harm I've done. The problem is too big. I should know – I've lived it for decades. Any impact I can have now would be too small. It's too late."

Ricky thought for a moment. The sound of the sirens and the growing roar of the fire made every second seem like an eternity, but he didn't see any other way.

"Dr. Nova, can I tell you a story?"

She didn't respond, but he continued anyway.

"A friend of mine named Monique told me a story once. It went something like this. There was once a racc..." Ricky coughed a little and corrected himself.

"There was once a human, a man, walking along the beach in the morning. He then saw a little girl throwing rocks on the shore. As he approached her, he realized that she wasn't throwing rocks, but actually flinging starfish back into the ocean.

'What are you doing?' he asked. The girl replied that the tide had brought the starfish there, and if they are left on the shore, the rising sun will dry them out and kill them.

The man looked around at all of the starfish that surrounded them. 'But there are so many of them. Hundreds. Thousands! You cannot possibly make a difference.'

The little girl carried on undeterred, picking up a starfish and looking at it. She then flung it far into the ocean where it broke the water with a splash.

'It made *all* the difference for that one.'"

Ricky waited for any response, but there was none.

"Do you understand?" he asked. "None of us can do it all. We can't save everyone. We can't bring back those who have been lost or taken. The animals who were killed here are gone, but you can make sure there aren't any brought in to replace them."

She still didn't respond. He needed to keep talking to hit the point home.

"It's the same everywhere," he said. "The meat on the grocery store shelves is from animals that will never breathe again – we can't help them. But we can stop the next animals from being killed if we stop buying it and creating the demand for more."

Still no response.

"Dead animals mounted on walls and made into clothes and car seats don't care what happens to them now – they no longer feel pain. But we can stop making and buying products that would necessitate the demand for a now living creature to suffer and be killed tomorrow."

Was this even helping? He wasn't sure. He tried to bring it back to Dr. Nova and her work. "There are other ways to do scientific research without harming or killing animals. You need to find out how and convince others to do the same. Just because that's how it was done before doesn't mean you need to keep doing it that way. Someone long ago made it "normal" to use animals this way, but it's not right when there are other options."

No response from Dr. Nova. The wailing sirens continued their screaming, probably annoyed that these two weren't heeding their call.

Ricky continued. "We can all see what's right and wrong and make a difference when it's right in front of us. We have to. You are right in front of me and I can save you. So that's what I'm going to do. Hopefully if I do save you, then you can save others. And for each one of them, it will make all the difference."

Ricky didn't know what else to say. He waited for a response, which finally came after a few moments.

"Are all firefighters this concerned about animals?" she asked coyly.

"Uh, maybe not all," he said with a muted laugh. "But I am. And I care about you as well. You are worth saving. I know that now. I hope you do too."

"I don't know," she replied. But I'd like to think I can be, with a little time."

Ricky heaved an audible sigh of relief. "Good! Let's get you out of here!"

It was then that she looked up at the voice coming from the vent and saw a fuzzy raccoon face staring back at her.

"What the…?" she said, backing up from the sink and mirror.

Ricky quickly slid backwards in the duct to hide from view.

"Is that… is that *you* in the duct?" she asked, getting closer again and trying to see into the recesses of the dark vent.

"Oh crumbs," Ricky said to himself. "Uh, yes, I'm here in the other room talking to you through the duct. Are you ready to go?"

"I thought I saw a face. A *raccoon* face in the vent," she said with disbelief. She was now trying to stand on the sink to get a better view.

Ricky tried to think quickly. "Uh, maybe there are some animals that were living in the attic or something and they are getting away from the fire. Forget about them for now, they are very smart and should be able to get out on their own."

"But this building doesn't have an attic…" she started to counter.

Ricky interrupted her hastily. "They are *really* smart actually. Did you know that raccoons are just as smart as monkeys and primates? In fact…"

A loud boom and subsequent crashes coming from the area of the fire interrupted them both. The structure of the building was starting to fail.

"Ok, ok, I'm ready," she said, getting back down onto the floor. "I want to get out of here."

"Yes, of course," Ricky said with relief. "Ok, get a bit more water on yourself and go back to the edge of your office and the animal holding area."

Dr. Nova soaked herself thoroughly again and went to the edge of her office. The flames from the main hallway were now well established and spreading rapidly to the ceiling and walls all around the doorway.

She looked down at Kim and held her hand out. "Shall we do this together, my tiny friend?"

Kim took her outstretched hand and climbed up to her shoulder, nestling under the wet lab coat.

"Hold on tight now," she said looking down at Kim's trusting eyes. Kim nodded in response, which made Dr. Nova pause for a moment with a small smile.

"Ok, I'm ready!" she said loudly in the direction of the vent.

"Alright," Ricky said. "The wet lab coat will help protect your skin from the heat and flames. Do you have any safety glasses you can put on? They might help protect your eyes a bit."

"Yes, one second," she said, shuffling some things around on her desk until she found them stuffed in an overturned coffee mug. She put them on quickly.

"Ok, got them."

"As you know," Ricky said loud enough for her to hear, "the flames in the main hallway are pretty intense. The wet lab coat won't be enough to protect you from all of that, so you will need to get that fire extinguisher and blast it as you go right through that doorway. It should be a CO2 extinguisher because of all of the computer equipment you have in here."

"Carbon Dioxide... that will come out really cold!" she said, remembering years of chemistry classes.

"Yes, exactly! You won't be able to put out the fire, but that doesn't matter. All we need is for you to create a little bubble of colder air that can protect you as you run through the flames. Go left and straight out the front door. It's propped open."

Dr. Nova was suddenly second guessing this idea. "Run through the flames. Great. That sounds like fun."

"Don't worry, you can do this," Ricky said, hoping he sounded more confident than he felt.

In reality, any number of things could go wrong. She could get horribly burned by the intense flames. She could inhale too much smoke and pass out, and *then* get horribly burned by the flames. Or she could accidentally inhale the CO_2, *then* pass out, *then* inhale too much smoke, and *then* get horribly burned by the flames.

He had to stop himself. "Focus on the positive Ricky," he said to himself. *Emma and Monique would be proud*, he thought with a smile.

"One more thing," he added. "Be careful not to inhale the CO_2 from the fire extinguisher. Take a few big breaths before you go to load up your body with oxygen, and then hold your breath as long as you can. Exhale slowly if you need to. The smoke is often more dangerous than the fire."

"Got it," she replied. She then started breathing as deeply as she could. It was very difficult though since the thick black smoke was spreading everywhere. After a few coughs she was able to get a few good breaths in.

Ricky continued with some tips as she was preparing herself. "This is it! Stay as low to the ground as you can and move quickly. Don't stop until you are outside of the building."

"Ok. I think I'm ready," she said as she trained her eyes on the red fire extinguisher case to the right of the door. She got herself into a crouched position, ready to sprint. Kim was holding tight under the dripping lab coat.

"GO! GO! GO!" Ricky yelled as loud as he could.

Dr. Nova took off in a flash, churning up debris of ceiling tiles and glass from the floor as she ran.

She crossed the span of the animal holding area quickly, not stopping to look at the empty cages or metal doors that swung wildly as the wind from her movement caught them.

She could feel the heat increasing with every leap as she got closer and closer to the flames from the hallway. The red case with the fire extinguisher was just off to the right of the doorway and getting larger quickly.

It would take too much time to slow down smoothly, so she slammed into the wall and the case with a crash. She instinctively pressed herself against the nearest animal cages to stay as far away from the flames and intense heat as possible.

If any further instructions were coming from the firefighter in the other room, she couldn't hear them anymore. But she didn't need them either – she had seen this fire extinguisher and others like it for years and had probably read the simple directions a hundred times.

She raised up her hands together and used her elbow to smash apart the scored plexiglass window on the front of the case. Large bits of clear plastic fell away quickly, and she grabbed the heavy red metal canister inside.

There was a circular metal pin on the side of the silver handles at the top. Hugging the canister with her left hand and arm, she used her right hand to rotate the pin clockwise, breaking the small plastic tie that held it in place. She then pulled the pin completely out of the handle and tossed it aside. Next, she grabbed the large black nozzle and pried it out of the collar that held it close to the red body. A short black hose allowed her to aim it. The extinguisher was now ready to fire.

Wasting no time, she squeezed the handle and released a billowing white cloud of super cooled carbon dioxide into the doorway and hallway. Normally you would aim at the base of the fire and sweep back and forth to try to put the flames out, but that wasn't what she was going for here. She simply needed to cool the area immediately around her enough so that she could pass through without getting burned.

White clouds filled the entire area and as wisps of it blew back at her she could feel the sudden change of temperature. Her wet clothes and hair even started to develop white crystals of ice. Now it was time to go through.

Keeping the handle of the extinguisher squeezed, she crouched as low as she could towards the floor and started to make her way through the doorway. Having worked here for years, she at least knew exactly where to go, even though she couldn't see much.

She pressed into the hallway and felt splashing water at her feet. Directly to her right was a wall of black and red that she fought back with her clouds of white as she kept moving in the opposite direction.

Then the fire extinguisher ran out. It had only been about ten or fifteen seconds, but soon it gasped its last breath in a small puffy cloud. The roaring wall of red flames and black smoke filled the void immediately.

The heat was overwhelming, and she could feel her eyes burn as the smoke crept past the sides of the safety glasses. She windmilled backwards and felt her back hit the floor with a splash. The now empty fire extinguisher hit the floor with a loud clang and rolled to a rest near the wall.

Seeing no other option, this seemed like a good time to run. She tried her best to bolt away from the fire and towards where she knew the front entrance to be.

Her feet slipped on the wet floor as she fumbled around in the dark, but she finally caught her balance and made some progress. With every step the heat was decreasing. She couldn't see the front entrance door but knew it wouldn't be long before she would be close.

It was then that the sudden and immediate need to breathe came upon her. She had been holding her breath, but with the effort of getting the extinguisher and scrambling down the hall, her body was now screaming for air.

She knew that she couldn't breathe in. The smoke was far too thick and might overpower her. She must keep going.

With every step she could feel her diaphragm and lungs spasming, trying desperately to do their job to expel CO_2 and intake oxygen. The only thing she could do was to exhale slowly, which would at least lower the CO_2 level a bit.

She pressed on further and further down the main hallway. Soon she saw a metal strip in the floor that marked the threshold from the tile in the hallway to the carpet in the entrance and lobby. Almost there!

Then she started to feel dizzy and a little confused as she got closer to the door. She was starting to see growing white spots filling her vision. There was something jammed into the front door that was propping it open. Was that a coffee mug? Or an umbrella? She reached out and clawed at it with her hand and wound up stumbling.

As she caught herself, without thinking she gasped for air and immediately started coughing and choking on smoke. Her hands outstretched in front of her, she gagged and tried desperately to breathe. All forward movement towards the propped door stopped as the need to breathe took priority over everything else. Her thoughts instantly got panicky and scattered. Nothing else matters when you can't breathe.

Then a wash of cool fresh air billowed past her, enveloping her entire body. She managed to breathe in a little at first, coughed some more, and then inhaled more and more fresh air. It smelled of fresh summer rain and cut grass.

A white flash of light and a deafeningly loud boom pulled her attention back to the door, where she saw Kim the monkey, holding the door open and looking at her with concerned eyes.

With her brain getting more oxygen now, her thoughts began to process more clearly. *The door. Go through the door. Get outside.*

Each new breath was helping. She managed to lift herself off of the floor and stumble forward through the doorway onto the concrete landing at the front entrance. She continued a few feet more until she collapsed in the grass to the side of the front walkway.

She tore off the safety glasses and took longer and slower breaths, coughing out the remnants of smoke and enjoying the feeling of the cooling rain drenching her and washing away the heat and soot. Her wet hands pulled at fistfuls of soft grass to make sure this was real.

It was. She had made it.

After a few long moments, she sat up and noticed Kim off to her side, peering at her inquisitively.

"Are you ok, my tiny friend?" she asked, holding out her hand towards the small monkey. The rain ran off of it in small rivers that ran down her arm.

Instead of taking the proffered hand, Kim looked back at the burning laboratory. Dr. Nova did the same, imagining what the little capuchin must be thinking.

"No, my friend. We aren't going back in there."

"Never again."

CHAPTER TWENTY-NINE: *AFTERMATH*

A bit later as the rain was finally subsiding, Randall Woodman was delivering Emma Gregor to the emergency medical team that had just arrived. Black soot and gray ash coated his thick protective gear. Small bits of retro-reflective patches caught the light and made it seem like his jacket and pants had a power source illuminating them. He was holding Emma in his arms and gave them the details as he got closer.

"I found her unconscious in one of the labs in there. There is a deep laceration to her left temple, and she might have a concussion. Maybe some smoke inhalation. She's just coming around now."

A female EMT ran right up to her and helped Randall lay her down gently on a padded gurney behind the ambulance.

"Miss, we're here to help you. Can you tell me your name?" she asked.

"Uh, Em. Emma," she said slowly.

"Ok, Emma. Do you know what year it is?" The EMT asked while checking her vitals.

"Yeah, um, it's 2019," she replied, looking around and waking up a bit more.

"Who is the President of the United States?" the EMT asked as she went through her standard protocol for head injuries.

"Uh, do I have to answer that?" Emma replied with a little giggle.

Randall coughed and looked cross but the EMT laughed.

"Yup, I think she's going to be fine. We'll get her right over to the hospital for a full workup and evaluation."

Randall started to turn away.

"Wait!" Emma said as they started to strap her in. They both paused and looked expectantly at her.

"I'm sorry Mr. Woodman. I shouldn't have said that. What I should say is this… thank you. From the bottom of my heart, thank you for risking your life to save me."

Randall's face softened and he smiled humbly. "Just doing my job. But you're welcome."

"Did all of the animals get out?" she asked cautiously.

"I think so," Randall said. "The rest of the unit finally went in after Hazmat cleared them. They said the front door was propped open and all of the cages were empty. Your friends over there must have let them all out."

Oh no! Emma's eyes went wide with surprise and concern for Ricky and the rest of the rescue team. Were they discovered?

"My… friends?"

"Yeah, the woman and the monkey," he said as he pointed to a dark-haired woman sitting on the edge of a short wooden fence that lined the road to the loading dock. She was wrapped in a gray blanket and was holding something small and furry. Another set of EMTs were tending to her.

"Is that your mom?" The EMT asked.

"No, just a friend."

"Don't worry, she's ok. You'll both be put together at the hospital". The EMT then collapsed the legs of the gurney and slid Emma into the back of the ambulance.

Randall's smile changed to a slight expression of confusion. "Wait, how did you know my name?"

"Oh," Emma said. "I must have seen it on the back of your jacket or something."

Randall didn't seem convinced.

"Uh, ok. Well, you get better and heal up," he said with a tip of his hat.

Emma smiled and gave a little wave as they secured the

gurney and closed the rear doors behind her. The ambulance then came alive with lights and sirens as it pulled away around the building and towards the main road.

Randall then walked to the truck where Rosco was tied to the bumper. He got down on one knee in the mud and looked into his eyes. After a moment he took off his oversized gloves and gave him a good fur scruffing on both sides of his neck. Then a few good pats on the head.

"Good boy, Rosco. You good boy."

Rosco replied "affirmative!" with a single bark and a few sloppy licks to Randall's face. His eyes were bright, and his tail was wagging like windshield wipers on the highest setting.

Randall then got up and walked towards the woman with the monkey to check on her. She had somehow gotten out of the building on her own and walked right over to the rest of the unit crew.

This had happened right about the time that he was inside the building looking for the animals that weren't there. But he did find that girl, and that definitely made the effort worth it. He shuddered to think what would have happened if he had stayed outside to wait like he was supposed to. One thing was for sure; this was a fire he would never forget.

He saw the woman look up as he approached. "Hi Miss, I'm Randall Woodman, one of the crew here. Are you ok?"

The woman got up quickly, set the monkey down gently and then threw her arms around Randall in a tight embrace.

"Thank you so much for helping us to get out of there!" she said sincerely.

"Uh, no problem," Randall said. He wasn't sure why her reaction to him was so strong, but maybe she was just glad they were here on the outside to pick her up and get her to the hospital.

She continued unabated. "It was tricky at the end there near the main door, but we made it. That fire extinguisher didn't last long, but it was just enough to get us out." She looked down at the small monkey as if to confirm her retelling of the story and the monkey seemed to smile back at her.

"Well, I'm just glad everyone made it out ok," Randall said as he looked over at the building that was still ablaze just behind the woman's back. With the additional crews on site using foam, the flames were finally starting to recede. The smell of burning plastic and noxious chemicals still hung in the air though and there were occasional pops and crashes from the structure.

"I'm so glad you got all of the other animals out. Did you see where any of them went?" she asked.

"Um, no, I'm sorry but I didn't see any of that," he answered.

"Well, it doesn't even matter. I'm just glad you got them out."

Randall was just about to ask what she was talking about when he noticed something moving near the side of the lab. At first, he thought maybe it was just a piece of debris that had fallen off of the roof. He rubbed his eyes a little to clear up his vision and saw that whatever it was, it was still moving.

A moment later it became clearer as it started moving away from the building. It looked somewhat like a very small person in a white lab coat. Maybe another researcher or lab technician they had missed? Did they hire children or something?

"Excuse me for a moment," he said while keeping his eyes trained on the moving mass.

"What in the blazes…?" he said softly to himself.

It had stopped moving about halfway between the side of the building and the outer perimeter fence and was looking right at him.

There was no mistaking; it was a raccoon wearing a white lab coat.

Masked face, ringed tail, the works. But it was standing upright on its hind legs more like a human. After a moment it pulled the sleeve back on its left arm and looked to be talking into a watch or wristband.

Randall just stood there, dumbfounded with his mouth open.

A second later, the raccoon turned back towards the fence and continued running with a slight hop in its step. It seemed to slide under the fence and quickly disappeared from view on the other side.

"Are you ok?" the woman asked, not having seen any of this that happened behind her.

"Uh, yeah. Fine. Great." His mind flashed back to the trail camera recording of the animals freeing Rosco from the trap. What do you say when you've seen something that you know you cannot have seen?

"What kind of work do you *really* do with the animals at this lab anyway?" he asked, not knowing what she would say.

The woman looked back towards the building with an odd expression in her eyes.

"The wrong kind."

Something about how she said it made him not want to ask any more questions.

"Ok, well, they should take good care of you at the hospital."

"Thank you again, Mr. Woodman. Your compassion for animals is inspiring," she said with obvious admiration.

"Um, sure. Good night," he said and started to turn to leave.

"Good night," she said. "By the way, you sound much different in person."

Randall turned back for a moment. "Um, ok," he replied, not knowing what else to say.

It was the weirdest conversation he could recall having in a long time.

CHAPTER THIRTY: *REFUGEES*

Ricky paused for a moment to reply to Jake. "Yeah, everyone's out. I'm about halfway to the fence. Oh crumbs! Randall Woodman is looking right at me."

"Well get a move on!" Jake replied through the wristband. "We'll meet you down the road a bit."

A few minutes later, Ricky saw the gray car pulled off to the side of the road and noticed a gathering of animals in a circular clearing in the woods just beyond. As he got closer, he saw Minka licking her fur, as well as Jake sitting on a tree stump in the middle with a few of the refugees from the lab below. More were in the trees and brush all around.

Minka paused her cleaning, Jake jumped down, and the three of them came together beside the stump. A faint glow from the fire and the crew's lights lit their furry faces. The roar of the flames was now being drowned out by the steady sound of katydids and crickets in the warm summer night. A few bright stars started to peek out in the sky above.

"We did it," Ricky said looking around. "I can't thank you enough. None of us could have done this on our own. But working together we saved them."

Jake looked thoughtful for a moment. "We really did. We made a difference tonight."

"Our Emma is safe," Minka said with a sigh.

At that moment, a black and white hooded rat walked up and addressed them as a group. The other rats, mice, rabbits, cats, dogs, and monkeys all watched from behind in a collected group.

"Excuse me, but we don't know what to do," the rat said.

"Do about what?" Minka replied, asking the question the three of them were all thinking.

"Anything," said the rat with innocent eyes. "We've never been out of the lab before. What do we do now? Who will take care of us?"

Ricky pondered for a moment. It was a serious question. He looked around the clearing at all of the various animals and proceeded to climb up onto the stump in the middle.

Ricky cleared his throat a little and then began.

"I come from a place where every animal is an equal," Ricky said loudly and with surprising authority. "Life can sometimes be difficult, but it's always our own. We make our own futures."

The rat was listening intently, as were the others. Occasional spatters of rain dripping from the leaves above made them blink, but they were rapt.

"The same now goes for you. All of you. There won't be a human taking care of you anymore, but they won't be experimenting on you either," he said as he looked back towards the lab.

He pointed out to all of them with both paws wide. "What happens now is up to you. I won't tell you what to do with your lives now as some directive or order. You have free will and can decide that for yourselves."

He paused to look down at the rat. "But you are not alone either. You have millions of years of evolutionary training right in your DNA. Find food, make homes, and create little fuzzy babies to share your lives with." There was a suppressed giggle from somewhere in the crowd.

"This is your new beginning. It might seem so unnatural at first to no longer have your lives controlled by another, but I assure you that you can do it."

Ricky looked all around the circle of animals again as he continued. "The one thing I will say is that you are better off together. We all have strengths and weaknesses. Myself included. We can survive on our own, but together we can thrive." Ricky looked down at Minka and Jake with a smile. They smiled back.

"All around you are the woods of Connecticut," he said, gesturing to the surrounding forest. "It will be hot in the summer and bitterly cold in the winter. Be prepared and listen to your instincts."

He gestured to Minka and Jake and himself. "Any of you who would like to come with us now are welcome to. There is a town nearby with houses and more regular sources of food from the humans. There are dangers too, but we can help teach you."

He pointed back to the road. "For any who would like to stay, just remember that this road leads to the town, and you will always have friends there."

Ricky looked back at the hooded rat to see if that answered the question. The rat nodded and smiled. "Thank you," it said with intense gratitude.

Jake then spoke up. "I'd like to add something," he said, jumping up on the stump next to Ricky.

Jake paused for a moment as if trying to find the right words.

"Try not to hate the humans."

Ricky was surprised to hear this from Jake but hid his reaction and let him continue.

"As you well know, some of them are terrible. Some treat animals like property and ignore the fact that we feel just like they do," he said to the crowd as he looked around and took in the scene.

"Some eat us. Some hurt us and kill us to wear our skins or just for fun. I lost my own dear love to one of them and the hatred that burned in my heart nearly consumed me," he said as he blinked away a stray drop of rain.

He looked very sad for a moment and continued. "But not all humans are bad. In fact, if it weren't for one human in particular, Emma Gregor, none of you would be here right now. She decided to come and do the right thing when we couldn't or wouldn't. She's the one that really saved you."

A monkey stepped forward from the crowd and spoke up. "Then we will honor her in this place. This is where our freedom begins, and she will be remembered. This will be known as Emma's Ring."

"Rightly so," Jake said as he nodded his head and pulsed his tail.

Minka then jumped up on the stump and joined Ricky and Jake in a soggy but wonderful hug. They all enjoyed a peaceful moment of hope and accomplishment there in the woods under the stars.

Minka was the first to break the silence. "I hate to be the one to end this beautiful moment here, but we need to get this car back before the hospital calls Emma's dad."

"Oh crumbs, you're right," Ricky said.

"I'm driving this time," Jake said with a wicked grin.

CHAPTER THIRTY-ONE: *MASON*

At the hospital, Emma and Dr. Nova found themselves in a room together, each with her own bed and monitoring equipment. It was late, but neither of them were sleeping. The room was a symphony of white and pale blue that seemed to glow in the moonlight coming through the window.

Emma didn't have fond memories of hospitals, so she was relieved to find her raccoon keychain in the pocket of her jeans next to the bed. She smiled at its tiny friendly eyes and thought of Mom. The smell of the hospital made her seem even closer.

"What were you doing at the lab?" Dr. Nova asked plainly, startling Emma and breaking the awkward silence. "Did you set the fire?"

"No! Of course not!" Emma replied, hiding the keychain away under the blanket the nurse had placed on top of her. "I was just riding my bike in the woods. I saw the fire and I figured I would try to help the animals to get out."

Dr. Nova wasn't convinced. "In the middle of the night? I don't buy that for a second. What were you really doing there? Are you an animal rights activist?"

Emma thought about it for a second. Before she could answer, Dr. Nova continued, softening her tone. "Don't worry – it's ok. Your secret is safe with me."

"I didn't set the fire," Emma said cautiously, "but I guess you could say I'm on the side of the animals. I hated the thought of them trapped in there."

"Yeah, me too," Dr. Nova replied as she looked down at the wires connected to her skin under the white gown with small blue accents on it. She thought of one of the monkeys in the lab and pushed the wires out of sight. "Won't your mom and dad be worried about you?"

Emma was quiet for a moment. "Mom's gone. But Dad will probably have a conniption fit."

"Sorry to hear about your mom," Dr. Nova said gently.

"That's ok, it's been quite a while," Emma said. "Dad's always telling me I need to get out more, so maybe he won't be too mad."

"I wouldn't count on that," Dr. Nova said with a laugh.

A few moments of silence passed.

"What will you do now that the lab is gone?" Emma asked.

"That's a really good question," Dr. Nova replied. "I'm done experimenting on animals, but my whole life has been training in research and animal biology. I'm not sure what else I can do."

"Yeah, I can see how that would be challenging," Emma said. An interesting thought then popped into her mind. "A friend of mine told me there is quite a future in lab-grown 'clean meat'. Have you heard of it?"

"Oh yeah?" Dr. Nova asked with intrigue. "Cultured animal proteins? I might have to look into that."

Before they could continue the conversation any further, they were interrupted by rapid footsteps coming down the hallway that were getting louder with each step.

Breathless and ragged looking, Emma's dad burst through the doorway and bee-lined in between the beds to hold Emma tightly in his arms.

"Emma, honey! Are you ok?" he said whilst checking her over like a shopper inspecting a melon in the produce section. His pale blue eyes were wide with concern and his blondish hair was disheveled as if he had just rolled out of bed.

"Yes, Dad, I'm fine," she said. "Just a small cut and some smoke inhalation. They said I can go home in the morning."

"Oh, thank goodness," he said with relief. But then his tone changed. "What in the world were you doing out there at that place? What were you thinking sneaking out at night? You could have been killed! Were you with anyone else?"

Emma wasn't sure how to answer any of those questions, so was quite relieved when Dr. Nova cleared her throat loudly to announce her presence in the room.

"Oh, I'm so sorry," he said apologetically. "I didn't realize anyone else was in here."

"That's ok," Dr. Nova replied. "Emma here was actually at the lab to help me with an important project. My intern quit suddenly, and her science teacher had recommended her. I'm sorry, it was an emergency."

Emma's eyes went wide as Dr. Nova singlehandedly seemed to save her skin. Dr. Nova turned towards her and gave a little wink.

Emma's dad then turned around to introduce himself and seemed to freeze in place when he saw her in the bed next to Emma's.

He noticed the faint touch of ash around the edges of her pale face, her long black hair, and her stunning smile. She was quite beautiful on the whole, especially given her present condition, but her piercing blue eyes were amazing. He was mesmerized.

"Dad? You ok Dad?"

"Um, sure honey. Sorry. Yes, I'm fine," he sputtered out.

Dr. Nova laughed a little and blushed.

"You know that we were the ones in the fire, right? Should we get you some oxygen or something?" Emma needled playfully.

"Ah, no. Thanks," he said trying to compose himself.

Dr. Nova held out her hand. "I'm Katie. Nice to meet you."

He took her hand and finally found his voice. "Emma's Dad. Nice to meet you too."

Katie arched one eyebrow alluringly. "Emma's Dad?"

"Oh, sorry. Mason. Mason Gregor."

"Nice to meet you, Mason," she said with a smile.

"Same here. I mean, nice to meet you too." He was suddenly finding English to be trickier than usual.

"May I have my hand back?" she asked playfully.

"What? Oh! Yes, of course," he said, recoiling a bit in an attempt not to seem creepy. Was it too late?

"So… Dad," Emma said trying to get his attention back, "they said you can come back for me in the morning and pick me up. We should probably rest up now." She figured the sooner they could end the conversation the sooner she could avoid too many questions about what had really happened.

Mason looked around the room and noticed an oversized recliner chair across from the beds. "That looks comfy, do you think I can stay here with you?" he asked. "I know you're probably ok now, but I don't want to let you out of my sight."

Emma leaned over towards Dr. Nova. "Dad's a bit of a worrier," she whispered in a not-so-whispery voice.

Dr. Nova smiled. "He loves you. No shame in that."

"Would it be ok with you?" he asked sheepishly of Dr. Nova.

She enjoyed torturing him for a few brief moments.

"Yeah, go on. Make yourself comfortable. But there's a price," she said.

"A price?" he asked curiously.

"Dinner," she said with a mischievous smile.

PART FIVE: THE DEPARTURE

CHAPTER THIRTY-TWO: *FAREWELL*

*T*he next morning was clear and bright. The storm had brought cooler temperatures and had filled the brook next to the shed to near overflowing. Water fell over the rocks with soothing sounds and wound its way in a twisty path away towards some unseen end beyond the trees.

Ricky had only gotten a few hours of sleep, but it was enough. A strange feeling of restless energy filled him as he opened the door of the shed and took in the wooded scene in bright sunlight. Ricky inhaled the sweet morning air like it was a precious gift. Dew laced the grass and moss on the ground as heavy tree boughs swayed gently in the breeze. It felt like Christmas morning or the day of a wedding.

But there was a tinge of sadness too.

His mission was complete, but he didn't want to leave. It had only been a short amount of time, really. But this felt like home. Emma, Monique, Jake, and Minka. Even Al, Randall, Rosco, and Dr. Nova were a part of his life now. Lush trees, fast cars, and vindictive squirrels. Huge trash pandas and rescued lab animals. It felt so strange to think in a few short hours he would be leaving it all behind.

He then heard a car pulling up into the driveway. A few minutes later, he saw some activity inside the house. Emma and her dad must have returned from the hospital.

Ricky waited for what seemed like hours. Eventually, he saw the back door of the house open up and Emma was walking out with something in her arms. Ricky ducked back into the shed in case her dad followed, but it was just Emma and whatever she was carrying.

Ricky's heart leapt as he saw that not only was Emma was headed towards the shed, but that she was also carrying Monique in her arms!

Both of them had bandages on their heads, as if they were trying to coordinate their outfits for the sake of fashion. Emma had a white bandage on the side of her head, whilst Monique had a patch covering her eye. Ricky pushed open the door to let them into the shed.

"Ricky?" Emma asked with a sweet voice as she ducked inside.

"Yes, I'm here!" he replied excitedly.

Emma put Monique down and knelt down on the wooden floor of the shed.

"Hi Ricky," Monique said with a big smile.

The three of them embraced in a warm and fuzzy hug that lasted more than a few minutes. The furry, smiling, and laughing ball of the three friends rolled around on the wooden floor as they squeezed each other and shed a few tears of joy.

"We made it!" Ricky exclaimed.

"Together again at last!" Monique replied.

"My friends," Emma said at last, brushing away a tear. "Wait, where is Minka?"

As if on cue, they turned to the sound coming from the flappy door on the other side of the shed.

"Minka!" Emma said as she ran over towards her.

Minka's forward motion stopped. "Now, don't go messing up my fur now, I spent all night licking…. AAHHHH!"

Emma scooped up the cat in a swift motion and hugged her tight. Minka seemed to give a token bit of protest for the sake of appearances, but then softened and melted into Emma's embrace.

"It's so good to see you again, sweetie," Emma said, showering the cat with kisses. A loud and rhythmic purring sound filled the shed as Minka's bright eyes closed contentedly.

"So what happened after I left you?" Ricky asked. Emma put Minka down and they all sat together in a tight circle on the floor.

"I don't remember all of it," Emma said as she distractedly touched the bandage at her temple. "I started to come to as I was being carried out of the building. I recall coughing, the searing heat, and suddenly being drenched with water."

"I'm so sorry I had to leave you. You were unconscious and I just couldn't carry you out," Ricky said regretfully. "I tried."

"Don't you think on that for one minute," Emma said firmly. "You did what you could, and we worked together to help the others. How did you get Randall to come in to get me?"

Ricky shook his head as if with disbelief. "I didn't think it was really going to work, but Jake told Randall through the radio that there were animals and maybe a girl in the building. The other firefighter laughed it off, but Randall actually stepped up and did something about it."

"Really?" Emma asked with disbelief.

"Yeah," Ricky answered. "I never would have thought he was capable of such compassion and bravery, especially after seeing what he did to Monique."

Ricky was deep in thought for a moment as he gazed towards nothing in particular. "You humans are a complicated and wondrous bunch."

Monique extended her paw to hold Ricky's arm as if to confirm her hope that Ricky would see the good in humanity.

Ricky turned towards Monique. "How are *you*? I feel like I haven't seen you in forever."

"I'm doing ok," Monique said cheerfully.

"What about your eye?" Ricky asked hesitantly.

Monique lifted the patch and revealed her eye underneath that now had a cloudy white appearance to it. "Well, this eye is pretty blurry now, but fortunately I've got the spare on the other side."

Ricky looked at her white eye and felt a pang of regret for not being able to do anything about it.

"Am I too hideous with this now?" Monique asked as she hugged her striped tail self-consciously.

"Not at all!" Ricky said quickly. "If anything, you are now more intriguing and beautiful."

Monique smiled and chattered a cute raccoon sound. She looked away and seemingly blushed a bit. That is, if you could see through the fur.

Ricky turned to Emma. "What happened once you left the lab?"

"Well, they ran me through all kinds of tests and asked me all kinds of questions. I tried to be vague on what happened and played dumb as much as I could."

"That must have been tough," Monique said in total jest. Ricky chuckled and translated for Emma.

"Hush, you!" Emma said with a hearty laugh. "Then they put me in a room with Dr. Nova overnight."

"Is she ok?" Ricky asked.

"Yes, she is fine. Smoke inhalation mostly," Emma replied. "Fortunately, I think my dad was pretty smitten with her. That's been keeping him from asking too many questions. She's coming over later tonight."

Ricky studied Emma's face to try to figure out how she really felt about her.

"Does that bother you? I mean, her getting close to your dad like that?" Ricky asked carefully.

"For a moment I wasn't sure what to make of it. Especially since we knew so much about her treatment of animals in that lab. But I think she's changed. I got the impression she won't be doing that kind of work anymore."

"I got that impression too," Ricky agreed. "But what about… your mom?"

"Yeah, I thought about her too. When I saw Dad making a fool of himself and fumbling trying to talk with Dr. Nova, all I could think was that Mom would have laughed. And she would have been happy to see him happy. I know I was."

Ricky nodded and smiled.

"What of Kim?" he asked.

"Who's Kim?" Emma asked with a tilt of her head.

"Sorry, I forgot you didn't meet her. Kim is a capuchin monkey that helped to get Dr. Nova back to reality enough to get her moving. Without her I don't think she would have gotten out."

"Yes, there was a monkey with her at the lab," Emma said, recalling the scene once she was outside. "I don't know what happened to her though."

"I do," Monique offered. "They brought her to the vet's office late last night. They said something about returning her to Dr. Nova once she was released from the hospital." Ricky relayed the message.

"Did you get all of the other animals out of the lab?" Emma asked.

"Yes," Ricky said with relief. "No pigs, but I don't think they survived the initial explosion. Everyone else is out."

"That's great to hear. But where are they?" Emma asked inquisitively. "There were a lot of them in that building."

"Some came back with us," Ricky said. "Others stayed in the woods. They wanted you to know how much they appreciate you saving them."

Emma smiled humbly. "Well, I only saved a few with you before I got knocked out. The rest were saved by you and the rest of the crew."

"No," Ricky said resolutely. "Everyone that was saved from that lab owes you their life. In fact, there are literally hundreds of animals in the woods right now singing your praises."

"Wow, that's pretty interesting," Emma said with wonder on her face. "So, I guess you completed your mission successfully after all?"

"Yeah, I guess I did," Ricky said. "I still don't know how saving these three targets will change the fate of the entire

228 | KENT GOLDEN

planet and the human race, but it's done, thanks to all of you."

"Glad to have helped," Emma said brightly.

Emma's demeanor then changed rather quickly. "So, does this mean that you will be leaving now?"

Ricky had a hard time even raising his gaze to meet Emma's. "Yes, I'm afraid it does," he said as he looked down at his wristband to check the time.

"I have about an hour left but have to head over the designated coordinates soon to make sure I am in the right place at the right time."

"We'll go with you then," Emma offered.

"As much as I'd love to spend every last minute with you all," he said, "I think it's better if I go alone."

"Why is that?" Monique asked quietly.

"Because…" Ricky began. He had to stop himself from choking up. "Because I think if you come with me, I won't be able to do it. I won't be able to leave."

Emma, Monique, and Minka sighed collectively and reached out for Ricky all at once to give him a hug.

"I'm going to miss you all so much," Ricky said with closed eyes that leaked tears at the edges. "I could never have done this without you, but more than that, I wouldn't have wanted to."

They released him slowly and he faced each one of them in turn. "You are my friends. Thank you for all that you have done."

"That's what friends are for," Monique said.

Minka nodded in agreement. "We'll miss you, trash panda."

Ricky's eyes brightened up at such an admission from Minka. "That means a lot to me."

"Will we ever see you again?" Emma asked with sadness creeping into her voice.

"I honestly don't know," Ricky said. "This has been such an adventure that I have a hard time thinking it can't continue on in some way. I truly hope this is not the end for us."

"I hope that as well," Emma said with a smile.

After a few moments of silence, Ricky took one last look around the shed and headed towards the door. Standing in the open doorway he ran his paw along the rough wood of the frame and squinted at the sunlight that was beaming in.

"Ricky, wait!" Monique called out.

Ricky turned and saw his three friends sitting there. Monique got up quickly and ran to the other side of the shed to where the white food cube sat. She opened it and took something out. Returning back to Ricky, she handed him a small parcel.

"For you. For the road," she said lovingly.

Ricky opened the white cloth wrapping and saw a small collection of his favorite black and white cookies, as well as a bunch of ripe red grapes. He held the package close and then pulled Monique in for another hug.

"Thank you, Monique. For everything," he said quietly in her ear. She squeezed him tight in response.

Summoning all of the willpower he could muster, Ricky forced himself out of the shed and into the yard.

He walked through the sun-dappled grass and padded across large bluestone steps in the pathway down the embankment towards the water. A warm breeze blew through his fur as he walked.

He entered the brook near where he had first landed and injured his leg. He gave his leg a little rub as if to see if it remembered all they had been through. The cool water felt wonderful on his paws as he crossed to the other side. The tall trees danced slowly in the wind above.

A little while later he checked the time and coordinates on his wristband. He was heading in the right direction and would be there in plenty of time. "As long as nothing else goes wrong that is," he said to himself.

At that moment his wristband gave a slight squeeze, notifying him that someone was approaching. He felt a small sense of apprehension as he heard a rustling in the ferns and plants nearby. A few seconds later he saw a few plants swaying with motion as a gray squirrel popped out.

"Jake!" Ricky said with a relieved smile. "I was wondering if I would see you again. Are you headed to the pickup coordinates to return to our time?"

Jake looked thoughtful for a moment. "No, I've decided to stay here. I didn't help as much as I should have with our mission, but maybe I can make up for it now by staying behind and doing what I can for the cause."

"Well, you never know, maybe they will send us on another mission." Ricky said, trying to be helpful.

"Maybe. But Isabelle is here too. I want to stay near her."

"I understand," Ricky replied solemnly. "So, this is goodbye then?"

"Yes, but I wanted to talk to you before you leave."

Ricky checked his wristband. "I don't have a lot of time, but maybe we can walk and talk?"

"Sure," Jake replied, taking his place at Ricky's side as he resumed the walk towards the pickup coordinates.

"I wanted to say that I'm sorry, Ricky," Jake said earnestly.

"Sorry for what?"

"For trying to sabotage the mission. I just couldn't get past the hatred I felt for Randall and Rosco," Jake said as he shook his head. "I let that change how I felt about all humans, without really giving them a chance."

"I understand," Ricky said as he climbed over a fallen tree in the woods. Jake leapt up onto it and then back down on the other side as if it weren't even there.

Ricky gestured to himself as if to take some of the blame. "I gave up on the mission too. I wouldn't have gone to save Dr. Nova if Emma didn't go. And we wound up saving hundreds of lives because of her courage."

"I know," Jake said. "Listen, about the mission, Ricky. There's something you should know," he said seriously. Ricky saw the look in Jake's face, and they stopped walking.

"What?" Ricky asked.

"Do you still have doubts about the mission?" Jake asked.

Ricky thought about it for a moment. "I confess… yes. I know we saved the three targets, Al, Rosco, and Dr. Nova, as well as some other animals who are no doubt grateful, but I still don't really see how that will change the fate of the entire planet and save the humans."

Ricky thought back to each target. "Al the butcher might make some changes in his life, but he's still running his shop that carries killed meat. Maybe Rosco and Randall will stop hunting and turn over a new leaf, but how will that change the world?"

Jake nodded and let him continue.

"As for Dr. Nova, maybe she can make a difference in lab research over time, but I'm still not sure how it all fits together. Why these three targets? How can it possibly make enough of a difference? I've been running it over and over in my mind, but I still don't have an answer."

Jake nodded in agreement. "As you know I've had the same doubts. Well, as the original mission leader I'm privy to information that you and Isabelle weren't allowed to see."

Ricky's interest was piqued, and he listened intently.

Jake continued. "I really did try to sabotage the mission and I thought I would never hear from the team in our time ever again, but this morning… I got a message."

"A message?" Ricky asked with curiosity.

Jake held up his wristband so that Ricky could see the display:

TARGET 01 – A. SMITH: COMPLETE
TARGET 02 – R. WOODMAN: COMPLETE
TARGET 03 – K. NOVA: COMPLETE

PRIMARY TARGET: COMPLETE

Ricky's masked face scrunched up a little as he looked it over. "What does it mean, 'Primary Target'?"

"It just showed up today – I had never seen it before. Go ahead and tap it," Jake said with a nod of his head.

Ricky reached out and tapped the display. A larger menu opened up with a photo of a middle-aged woman and some text below it that read "INFLUENCE ACCOMPLISHED".

"Who is she?" Ricky asked, puzzled about what this was all about. "I've never seen her before."

"Look closer," Jake said.

Ricky moved in to inspect the photo of the woman. She had brown hair with streaks of gray, greenish eyes, and shoulder-length hair. He did not recognize her. She was dressed sharply in a professional office setting of some kind. The room was formally decorated with light colored walls, long drapes in front of tall windows, and he could see that she was leaning against a large wooden desk.

Ricky squinted his eyes to see the framed photo that was sitting on the desk next to some papers. He reached out his paw and spread his fingers to zoom in.

It was at that moment that his mouth dropped open and his eyes lit up. "That's me! And Monique! That was the picture that Emma had taken at the picnic!"

Ricky looked over at Jake for a moment. Jake nodded his head in confirmation.

Ricky swiped back to the woman in the photo and instantly knew who it was.

"Emma!!"

His mouth hung open while his brain tried to process it all.

She was older and looked a bit different, but now he could see clearly that it was her. He even saw a small pale scar on her left temple. That must have been from her injury in the lab.

"But why would she be the primary mission objective?" Ricky asked.

"I don't know," Jake replied. "For some reason she will be important to the future of the planet. So… maybe that's why we had to save Al, Rosco, and Dr. Nova. Not because they are in themselves that important but because…"

"It's all about Emma!" Ricky said.

He thought more about the influence he had on her through the mission. Emma was there every step of the way, learning about how animals and humans might share the planet in better ways. She too had accepted things as they were because that's what was "normal" for her. It's how she was raised.

But through Ricky and the mission she was learning about the possibilities of compassion and understanding. She learned how things could be if only the humans would decide to change.

Al and Rosco and Dr. Nova might go on to change their own lives, but now Ricky could see how that would be secondary to Emma's experience with them. His meeting Emma, what he had thought was just happenstance, must have been calculated very carefully.

Through the saving of Al, she learned about animals being used as food sources when they don't have to be. Through Rosco she learned about hunting for needless sport and fashion. Through Dr. Nova she learned about animals being bred and tortured in the name of science. Each one offered a glimpse into the current world of human and animal relations.

Every step of the way she was learning to question the status quo and to think of better alternatives. *That* is why these three targets were chosen. *That* is why the mission needed to succeed. It was Emma all along.

"Wow," Ricky said. At first it was all he could manage. Then a thought occurred to him.

"Wait, does that mean they dropped me and broke my leg on purpose?!" he said with mock anger.

"I don't know, but I wouldn't rule it out," Jake said, shaking his head with either admiration or disbelief. Maybe both.

They laughed together like old friends.

Then another, darker thought occurred to Ricky that gave him pause. "If that is true, then does it also mean that they knew…"

"Knew what?" Jake asked.

Ricky exhaled and looked away for a moment. "Do you think they knew what would happen to Isabelle?" he asked hesitantly, unsure if he should even mention it.

After a few moments, Jake surprised him with a question in return. "Your leg. Was it worth it?"

"What do you mean?" Ricky asked.

Jake gestured to his leg. "Knowing what you now know about the mission and what it took for all of these different pieces to fall into place, was it worth it to you to endure the pain of your leg for the success of the mission?"

Ricky looked at his leg thoughtfully, knowing where Jake might be headed with this. "Yes, it was worth the pain," he said.

Jake responded. "Well, there's your answer."

"But this is a leg, not a life!" Ricky protested. "And it will heal. Do you think Isabelle still would have come here if she knew?"

"I know Isabelle," Jake said with a grin. "This mission was everything to her. She knew what was at stake and she was ready to sacrifice anything to see it done. I think she would have done it even if she knew what was going to happen."

Ricky found himself struck with admiration. "You are both amazing. It has been a privilege to serve with you."

Jake pulsed his fuzzy tail a few times. "And you, my friend."

Ricky then looked at his own wristband. "Ah, I need to get going."

"Yes," Jake said. "But I'm glad I caught you before you left. You needed to know."

"Thank you, Jake. We did it together," Ricky said.

"Yeah, I guess we did. 'Till our paths cross again."

They embraced for a moment and held each other at arm's length with mutual admiration.

"Take care, my friend." Ricky said. He then started to continue his walk towards the pickup location.

"Oh, one more thing." Jake said.

Ricky paused and turned around to face him.

"I got another message this morning after the mission summary," Jake said in a somewhat hushed tone as he looked around quickly. "I'm not supposed to tell anyone the details, but let's just say you might want to keep your wristband handy. You never know what the future might bring."

"I will indeed," Ricky said with a smile.

With that, Ricky the time traveling trash panda continued his walk into the woods and the new future that waited beyond.

CHAPTER THIRTY-THREE: *CHORKISH*

It had been a few weeks since Ricky had left, and Emma Gregor was learning how to adapt to her new reality. She could no longer hear animals talking, since the wondrous wristband went back with Ricky to the future, but she felt closer than ever to them all. Minka and Monique were practically inseparable, and Rosco would come by with a gray squirrel pretty often that must have been Jake.

Things were different at school now too. She had survived a raging inferno and saved the lives of a few hundred animals. She found it was no longer that difficult to simply speak up in class. She also decided to get more involved to try to improve things for animals wherever she could.

She was now on the student advisory board for her school, and they were pretty receptive to some of the ideas she was pitching. The yearbook was slated to have a leather cover to make it more "premium", but Emma was able to find a synthetic ultra-suede that felt even nicer and required no animals. Less expensive too.

The dead frogs for the biology lab were out as well. Augmented reality dissection apps were in, with a generous donation from local animal expert Dr. Katie Nova for digital tablets. Emma and her dad had floated the idea to her last weekend in the park, and she had gladly agreed.

Today's event in the school cafeteria would be an interesting one. For the last day of school before summer vacation, she had convinced the board and school administrators to let her do a blind taste testing of a meat alternative. She had a table full of small paper plates laid out, each one holding two halves of a chicken sandwich. One half was "real" chicken (or whatever animal Chorkish was really made out of), and the other half was the vegan alternative. The letters A and B were marked on the plates under the sandwich halves.

Behind the table were two large poster boards that showed some information about each choice. The animal meat side showed the hatching of a baby chicken, a few snapshots of life on a factory farm in terrible conditions, and a black box that had "CENSORED" written over it in large letters.

The school was adamant they wouldn't allow a photo of chickens being killed, even though that's the reality of it. But she hoped that everyone would get the idea. There were also numbers for the amount of water, energy, land, and feed needed to raise chickens to be slaughtered for a year's worth of Chorkish patties. Additional charts showed CO_2 output, pollution, and nutritional information like cholesterol and fat content.

On the other poster board, there were similar photos that showed the path of the plants and vegetables needed to make the vegan patties. There were no animals involved. Rows of green plants and ripe vegetables with vibrant colors stood in stark contrast to the grim conditions of the poultry farm. Again, there were numbers and charts for everything needed to make a year's worth of patties.

Looking at the data as presented, it was apparent that the "real" chicken patties were far worse for the chickens, the planet, and even the humans that were consuming them. The alternative vegan patties were absolutely the winners on paper.

But Emma knew that people are funny. They might want what they think of as "real" just because that's what they are used to. Chorkish was the incumbent and reigning champ. It needed to be a blind tasting to really find the winner. Katie and her dad had suggested a double-blind tasting, so that even

Emma didn't know which labels pertained to which option. That would prevent bias. She was too nervous to even try them herself, so she honestly didn't know which was which.

At the bottom of the two posters was some text written in large letters that spanned both boards:

Taste both sides! If you can't tell the difference, what does that tell you?

There was also a ballot box with small slips of paper so that everyone could vote for their favorite anonymously. Students crowded around and were stuffing their ballots into the box while horking down both options.

Fortunately, the table and her displays were very popular throughout the entire lunch period. Free food is always a winner!

But, after a while, she heard a few grumbles and what seemed to be a growing consensus that yes, they could tell the difference, and many preferred the taste of side "A", which was the "real" meat. A few students acted as expected and dramatically asked for bacon on top and some burgers too. The votes were stuffed in the box to be tabulated by the staff later.

Emma continued her day and anxiously awaited the big reveal that the principal would make just before the final bell. She was starting to feel a little disheartened and was second-guessing the entire idea.

Finally, the announcement happened just minutes before everyone would be released for the summer.

A tone and a crackle of static came through the small speaker near the door and the clock. A moment later they all heard the voice of the principal.

"Thank you to all who participated in today's special taste test in the cafeteria. We have tabulated the votes and we have a clear winner. By an overwhelming margin, students preferred choice "A.""

A number of students high fived each other and nodded knowingly that their choice had won.

The principal continued. "The faculty and staff also participated in a separate vote, and our winner was *also* for choice "A"."

Emma rubbed at the scar on her head distractedly and braced for the bad news.

"It would appear that, thanks to our own Emma Gregor, we will be having a change to our cafeteria menu!"

Emma's eyes lit up as she heard playful gasps from the students all around her.

The announcement continued. "Choice "A" was the vegan alternative meat. No animals were harmed to make it, it is better for the planet, and it is better for our own bodies as well. Congratulations on voting for this new menu item."

The final bell then rang and with excited cheers everyone got up from their desks and poured out into the hallway.

Emma packed up her books and notebooks in her backpack that now had a cute raccoon patch on it with the text "Save the Trash Pandas" in large friendly letters.

Billy, the frog eyeball bouncing lab partner from ages ago leaned in as he passed by on his way to the hallway.

"Long live the new Chorkish!" he said enthusiastically while pumping his fist in the air.

Emma laughed and smiled. "Score one for the animals," she said quietly to herself as she thought about what her next project might be. Swapping fresh veggies for pepperoni on the pizzas might be an option…

In the hallway her new friend Lexi put her hand on Emma's arm as they passed each other headed in opposite directions. "Congratulations you! We still on for tomorrow night?"

"Yup!" Emma replied cheerfully.

It was strange looking forward to school and spending time with other humans her age, but she was getting used to it.

CHAPTER THIRTY-FOUR: *THE SHOP*

Outside of the school, Emma hopped on her bike and enjoyed the ride home in the bright sunshine. The sky was blue, and the birds were chirping. The trees looked full and swayed in the gentle breeze.

As they often did, Emma's thoughts went to Ricky and she wondered what he might be up to now. She imagined he might be on other important missions to rescue animals and help people and the planet. She dearly hoped to see him again.

She was mid-daydream when she realized that she almost forgot to stop by Al and Bob's shop to pick up burgers. As she did nearly every night, Katie was coming over for dinner, and Emma was tasked with getting the provisions.

Emma thought about Katie coming over and how happy her dad had been recently. It was silly really that she didn't just move in. They were obviously in love, but she thought maybe they were taking things slow for her sake.

She appreciated the thought, but it was unnecessary. They were becoming a family regardless of sleeping arrangements.

Emma opened up the door and heard the familiar banter of Al and Bob going on at peak volume. She crept in slowly and ducked behind the bread aisle so as not to interrupt the show.

"I'm telling you, Al. I *know* what I saw! As plain as the nose on your face I saw it. It was a monkey! Right there on top of the dumpster."

Al was cleaning up the counter as Bob was opening boxes in the back room and yelling out his story. Al had recovered from his medical emergency and was now looking great. Emma barely recognized him in fact. He must have lost a bunch of weight and was just glowing with energy.

"Bob, that's just not possible. Maybe it was a skinny cat or something," Al said, obviously not persuaded. He continued to straighten up the knives and the area with the cheese cutters.

Bob was adamant. "Do you think I'm not able to tell the difference between a darned skinny cat and a monkey? It was a monkey! Like put a little hat on it and give it an organ grinder kind of monkey!"

Emma decided to move towards the counter slowly and Al suddenly noticed.

"Heeeyy! Look who it is!" he said cheerfully. "Bob, come see! This little monkey just walked right in the front door," he said with a snicker.

Emma held in her laughter as Bob popped his head out with angry eyebrows and a scowl like something out of a comic book. His faced lightened up immediately when he saw it was her.

"Emma! Good to see you love. Sorry for the yelling, you know how we are."

"Yup, I know," she said with a chuckle. "Still love you both."

Bob smiled broadly and disappeared to the depths of the back.

"What'll it be kiddo?" Al asked brightly, clapping his hands together and then spreading his arms out wide to show off all of the various foods on display. "We have lots of new vegetarian and vegan options."

"Hmmm… what's in your veggie burgers today?" Emma asked while looking at them in the case.

"Why?!" Al asked loudly. "Did they move? Ha!" He laughed heartily and Emma joined him with a chuckle and an indelicate snort that she covered with her hand.

"But seriously," Al said leaning in closer as if divulging a precious secret, "I just made them today and they are fabulous. The usual recipe that I know you like is the base, but I added a dash of cayenne pepper to them, so they have *just* the right amount of spice and flavor."

"Sounds great. I'll take four please."

"Four! You and your dad feeling hungry tonight?" he asked playfully.

"Well… Katie will be over again, and I also wanted to get an extra one for my friend Monique. She loves your recipes."

"Oh yeah? Well, tell your friend Monique she has good taste!" he said with satisfaction.

"I will indeed," Emma said. "I hope you don't take offense, but she's actually a raccoon. She's kinda one of the family."

The mood suddenly changed. Al paused for a moment as if pondering something very important.

"A raccoon you say?" he asked quietly. His face had an unusual expression on it that Emma couldn't quite place.

Emma suddenly felt as if she shouldn't have said anything. "Yes… I'm sorry. Please don't take offense. Like I said, she's one of the family. But we can just do the three burgers."

Al blinked and brightened back up as if the momentary pause hadn't happened.

"None taken, little lady. I'm giving you five for the price of three. Hers are on me."

"Why, thank you! That's very generous," she said.

"Don't mention it," he said as he leaned in close. "Especially to Bob back there," he said while pointing his thumb to the back of the store.

"Mums the word," Emma said with a zipping motion across her lips.

Al smiled and handed her the white parcel with yellow tape filled with the veggie burgers. She paid him and bowed her head a little in thanks. Then she headed to the front door.

Just before leaving she turned around. "By the way, Al,

you're looking great lately. New diet?"

"Yeah, something like that," he said with a smile.

"Something like that."

EPILOGUE: THE OFFICE

COURAGE
is
Resistance to Fear,
Mastery of Fear,
Not Absence of Fear.

- *Mark Twain*

*E*mma Gregor was staring out of one of the three tall windows of her office. The squirrels outside were chasing each other as they were collecting acorns from the large oak trees. Rich red and brown leaves fell around them as they played and foraged in the crisp autumn air. She pushed one of the colorful flags out of the way to get a better view.

One squirrel in particular had amassed an impressive collection of acorns in a pile and was bouncing around it as he was looking for good hiding spots. He seemed to look around to ensure no one else could see him and then dug a small hole swiftly. After another quick glance around, he rolled one of the acorns in, and proceeded to cover it back up with dirt.

Emma laughed a little to herself as she saw him compacting the dirt with his tiny paws, imagining what he might be thinking.

"They will *never* find that one," she said with a giggle.

Emma turned from the windows and sat at her desk. She had an incredibly busy day ahead, but like every other day, she made sure to ground herself first. It was always worth a few minutes of time, no matter how much lay ahead on the agenda.

Picking up her coffee mug, she sipped gingerly at the hot cappuccino. Nikki, her personal secretary, knew just how she liked it – foamed oat milk on top with a sprinkle of cinnamon.

She turned the mug around and looked at the illustration on it. It was a white mug with a raccoon in a cute red and green scarf. Nikki knew that on really important days, Emma would want this particular mug. It probably seemed silly, but Emma didn't care what anyone thought about that. It was important to her, and that's all that really mattered. She took another sip and enjoyed the comforting warmth.

The raccoon on the mug seemed to look at her with a hopeful expression. It made her think of Ricky.

Putting the mug down, she reached across the large desk and picked up the framed photo from that picnic so many years ago. She looked at Ricky and Monique and smiled. So many times, it seemed almost like an impossible dream. Other times it felt like yesterday.

Today, she could almost hear Ricky's voice and feel his fur.

She closed her eyes and had to take a deep breath to stop any tears from falling. She put the photo back on the desk and made an effort to look around the room to find something else to focus on.

Next to the picnic photo there was another framed scene of her dad and Katie at their anniversary dinner. She smiled and wondered when she might see them next.

Taking a short walk around the oddly round room, her eyes fell upon a small wooden plaque on the wall that she had painted herself a short while before being elected to this office.

Courage is resistance to fear, mastery of fear, not absence of fear. – Mark Twain

Today was a good day to see this. Years of preparations were at stake in today's meeting. Delegates from all over the world would be in attendance, and the issue at hand was a sweeping climate resolution that would affect every country in the world. By extension, it would affect every living creature on the planet as well.

Experts had analyzed in detail every major aspect of human activity and recommendations had been established.

They would be discussing binding policies on energy, animal welfare, resource allocation, food production, and various scientific and economic practices. It had become very apparent that all of these areas are connected, and that the United States must lead the way in changing the status quo.

She was confident, but also terrified. Every defeat over the years made her want to give up and hide. But she persisted, because she knew the cause was just. Soon she would know if this would be another defeat, or perhaps finally the victory she had so longed for.

Snapping back to the tasks at hand, Emma looked at her watch. It was almost time. She had to make sure she had everything ready. She walked back to the desk and took another quick sip from the raccoon mug. She picked up her pen and binder with her talking notes. That should be everything.

Just then, something made her think of her mom. What would she think of the life that Emma had lived? She opened one of the drawers of her desk and pulled out a very worn and faded raccoon keychain. She gave it a gentle rub and looked into its cute eyes.

"I miss you Mom," she said longingly.

For some reason, she imagined Ricky's voice telling Emma that her mom would be proud. She smiled.

Suddenly there was a knock at the door. She gave the raccoon keychain a kiss on the nose and put it next to the two photos on the desk.

"Thank you, Ricky," she said softly with a little sniffle.

She inhaled deeply and brought her attention back to the room and the present moment.

"Come in," she said assertively.

The door opened and Nikki poked her head in. Emma thought she saw one of the office cats run past in the background.

"It's time, Madam President," Nikki said. "They are ready for you."

"They had better be," she said with a grin as she strode across the Oval Office, past the intricate eagle symbol on the floor and then through the doorway.

"Today we choose the right path."

THE END?

ABOUT THE AUTHOR

Kent Golden is a professor living in southern Connecticut with his wife, Christine, and their three cats, Minka, Dax, and Newton. In addition to the inside animals, Kent and Christine enjoy tending to all of the wildlife in the area, including of course, raccoons.

Though they haven't been spotted lately, Ricky and Monique were real raccoons that would always travel together and visited Kent and Christine almost nightly for many years. Ricky really did walk with a limp and Monique really did have a cloudy eye. They absolutely loved Oreo cookies and grapes.

If you enjoyed this book, please consider rating it online and sharing it with others! Together we can choose the right path.

To see photos of the animals that inspired this book and to learn how to help animals in your own life, please visit:

www.TrashPandaBooks.com

ACKNOWLEDGMENTS

Heartfelt thanks to all who made this book possible, especially:

Christine Golden
Karen Golden
Neha Bawa
Echo Chernik
Alan Rice
Quinnipiac University
Sarah Rodgers
Hillary Drumm
Lor Ferrante Fernandes
Michele Cohen
Cathy McDowell
Laura Brewerton

www.TrashPandaBooks.com

CPSIA information can be obtained
at www.ICGtesting.com
Printed in the USA
LVHW042249020320
648721LV00005B/531

9 781714 368358